Lucy Holt
Gets Involved

MARK DAYDY

Previously published as 'The Patron of Lost Causes'

This is a work of fiction. All names, characters, locations and incidents are products of the author's imagination, or have been used fictitiously. Any resemblance to actual persons living or dead, locales, or events is entirely coincidental.

Copyright © 2020 and 2021 Mark Daydy

All rights reserved.

No part of this book may be reproduced, or stored in a retrieval system, or transmitted in any form or by any means, electronic, mechanical, photocopying, recording, or otherwise, without express written permission of the author.

Cover design by Mike Daydy

ISBN: 9798744756727

CONTENTS

1	News From Sussex	1
2	Birthday Girl	6
3	Jane	15
4	Old Haunts	24
5	The Silver Chalice	31
6	Taylor's Antiques	40
7	Going After the Bad Guys?	47
8	Train of Thought	55
9	There's a Man Called Francis	61
10	The Junior Partner	69
11	Brighton	78
12	What Am I Bid…?	88
13	The Chichester Connection	97
14	Eddie's Photos	103
15	Now What?	111

16	Lunch With Jane… and Nick	119
17	The Dynamic Duo	129
18	The H. S. Factor	135
19	Sunday Morning	141
20	A Picnic on a Hill	147
21	Two Mad Mornings	155
22	A Bit of a Shock	165
23	Money Talks	175
24	Lucy's Next Move…?	184
25	Hello Again	190
26	Lucy's Mistakes	197
27	Virginia	204
28	Frankie's Way	212
29	And What Do You Believe?	221
30	Surprises	226
31	More Surprises	233
32	So…	238

1

News From Sussex

The phone call that would shove someone else's crisis into Lucy Holt's uneventful mid-life came one evening in late August.

She was at home at the time, watching a single serving fisherman's pie and a small box of fries rotating slowly in the microwave. For some reason, it reminded her of that end-of-the-party dance she had with her boss last Christmas.

Oh, to be capable of whizzing and fizzing across a shiny dance floor like the celebs and professionals on TV. But it was several months since she last attended her keep fit class. Whizz and fizz? More like wheeze and fizzle out.

Her phone rang, bringing her back to the here and now – her fifth-floor abode in Barnet, north London. A quick glance at the screen told her it was Eleanor Ranscombe, an imperious aunt who lived in West Sussex.

"Hello?" answered Lucy, pretending she had no idea who was calling.

"It's Aunt Eleanor," said a refined voice that could easily have belonged to a member of the Royal Family.

"Hello, Eleanor. Is everything alright?"

"Good news. I'll be hosting a party for Libby's birthday."

"Oh." It was hard to distinguish this kind of good news from terrible news.

"She'll be seventy," Eleanor added.

"Seventy? Right…"

With the phone pressed to her ear, Lucy wandered into the lounge for no reason other than it provided a vague sense of fleeing.

"Lucy? You'll come down to Sussex, won't you?"

"Yes, of course. When is it? I mean, obviously on her birthday, but…"

"It falls on a Thursday this year."

"A Thursday?"

"Yes. Jane's coming."

"Jane? Yes, okay. No problem." She stared at her three-item collection of antiques on a shelf beside her imitation fireplace. "Are you sure you need to host it? I mean it's good of you, but I'd be happy with a glass of wine at Libby's."

"It's no trouble at all. And this way we can make sure everything runs smoothly."

Lucy absently picked up a small silver vase.

"Right. Yes. Well… thanks for the invite."

"I've got a few more people to call. Could I leave Victoria to you?"

"Yes, of course," said Lucy, even though her twenty-year-old daughter, Victoria, was more likely to visit Mars than Eleanor's house.

After the call, Lucy retrieved the fries from the microwave and gave the fisherman's pie a further three minutes by itself – also a reminder of Christmas, when her boss left her twirling mid-dance to answer a text.

As she picked at the fries, she thought of the Howard sisters – her long-departed mum, Sylvia, along with dictator Eleanor and lovely Libby. According to Lucy's cousin, Jane, daughter of the despot, the Howard girls had been raised to represent the *crème de la crème* of West Sussex society. Prim and proper. Upstanding. No unnecessary displays of emotion. The pay-off came as young women, when they triumphantly confused the 1960s with the 1860s.

She thought back to Libby's late husband, Eddie, drunkenly suggesting that teenage Lucy and Jane have some adventures before they were too old. They took the advice, but it didn't end well.

A few minutes later, at the kitchen table, she poked her fork into nuclear hot cheese-topped mashed potato. Not wishing to risk a scalded tongue for a second night running, she put the cutlery down and went to the window.

In the street below, life went on. Cars drove by. People crossed from one side to the other.

Oh no...

The Volkswagen with twelve doors was pulling up opposite. At least, that's what it sounded like to anyone not in visual contact. The man got out, slammed the door, went to the back, opened it – fiddle-fiddle, slam – and then returned to the front. Now his partner got out. Slam. She went to the back, opened it – fiddle, slam – and then returned to the front. Now they both opened their respective front doors again, reached inside – fiddle, fiddle – and withdrew. Slam-slam.

Lucy turned back into the room and thought about West Sussex, where she had lived until her twenties.

Slam.

She and her older brother, Richard, were from

Hallbridge, a village not far from the glorious South Downs. She would be going back now to the nearby market town of Camley to celebrate Libby's milestone with a small glass of dry sherry and a cucumber sandwich.

She glanced out of the window again. The couple had disappeared into their townhouse, no doubt to open and slam various doors.

It would be good to get away, she supposed. Not that she needed a break. Being the reception manager at a theological college was a most rewarding job – one she had held down for the past six of her ten years there. Not that she was religious. You didn't need to be religious to be part of the admin team. She just liked being around religious people. They were always polite and never caused any trouble.

Lucy returned to her meal.

For Libby's sake, she would go to Sussex. Her life in London wouldn't be too disrupted by it. Okay, she had no social life. Big deal. Plenty of people survived without doing lots of things with others.

While she ate, she enjoyed a cat video shared by Abigail, a non-religious work colleague. Abigail shared almost everything she did. If you got lucky, or liked lots of her stuff, you would get an invite to join her WhatsApp group where she would share her life and thoughts in more detail. Lucy was a member but not an enthusiastic one. She never shared anything herself online these days, whether it be nostalgia, shoes, relationship gossip, or microwaveable meals.

After dinner, she watched some TV – edgy Max was due to meet sensible Felicity for an elicit get-together. They wouldn't fall into bed, would they? Max was an insensitive oaf, but, on another level, Felicity needed to bloom as a human being.

Lucy's attention was drifting though. Even as the would-be lovers pouted at each other in close-up, the forthcoming party in Sussex came back to her.

Poor Libby.

Then Uncle Eddie's suggestion of teenage adventures interrupted her thoughts once more. That whole business with Greg.

It was thirty years ago. Watch the TV.

Lucy sighed. It was all long-buried history.

Of course, Cousin Jane rode it out back then.

Lucy had always suspected her cousin was one of those people who could appear on the front page of the newspapers, featured in a scandal, and still sleep soundly at night. It seemed that way at least. Not that Jane had ever been on the front page of a newspaper – although they did once both appear inside the Sussex Chronicle as part of a young teen choral ensemble at the county show. Those were the brilliant years. Lucy and Jane. Thirteen, fourteen, fifteen, sixteen. Almost hourly, it felt like they were growing in potential and promise.

She tried another channel. A penguin documentary.

So… she would be going to Sussex, where she would see Jane. Of course, the incident wouldn't be quite so long-forgotten then. It would resurface and become alive in the present. And any desperate on-the-spot attempts to rebury it would be shallow and easily dug up.

So perhaps she wouldn't go to Sussex for the party.

And yet she knew she ought to because she was forty-bloody-seven.

2
Birthday Girl

Lucy endured the Thursday morning train journey down to Sussex. She had planned to read a few chapters of a dark crime thriller set in Los Angeles, but a twenty-something couple across the aisle were revealing their intentions in the kind of giggly whispers that made it impossible to concentrate.

"No, Jonno… giggle… not here…"

Lucy was as broadminded as the next person but wondered if it was time the train companies introduced a separate carriage for randy co-workers heading to a conference. Especially those who giggly-revealed a hotel room booking even though they wouldn't be staying overnight.

Somewhat unexpectedly though, as she tried to shift her concentration to the glory of the early September countryside, the giggly whispers stirred a memory. It took a moment for the years to fully peel away, but there it shimmered, a train journey with her cousin…

Lucy was eleven, Jane, ten, and they were Brighton bound with their parents. On the strict understanding that they behaved, they had been allowed to sit by themselves farther up the carriage. Jane broke their pledge as soon as she set eyes on a couple who were "obviously having an affair". She went on to explain how the man would be "only interested in one thing". Observing the woman's pack of puffy pink sweets, Lucy whispered that the "one thing" in the man's mind might be getting his hands on her marshmallows. Jane giggled until she almost passed out.

*

Around ten-fifteen outside the station in the sizeable market town of Camley, Lucy took a taxi. Her next stop would be the Prince Regent Inn, three miles away in the large-ish village of Hallbridge.

Her original plan to attend the lunchtime party and be back home for dinner had fallen by the wayside. Chats with her daughter, Victoria, had led Lucy to commit to exploring some of her childhood haunts. It was her own fault – built on years of regaling Victoria with endless happy stories. Lucy's father's funeral of a few years ago had been too fraught for any such nostalgia trip. And she missed Eleanor's seventieth of two years ago with a bout of flu. But now…? It was a rare opportunity, she supposed. She could skip over any unpleasant memories in much the way she did when talking with her daughter.

As planned, Lucy arrived at the pub-hotel at half-ten. It was stylish, but clearly hadn't had much money spent on it. Shabby chic? Wasn't that a thing? Not that she was complaining – with the school summer holidays over, the room was half the price it had been the week before.

With two hours to spare before the party, Lucy took a welcome chance to acclimatize to Sussex with her thriller and a steaming mocha in the seating area overlooking the rear garden. Within ten minutes, she was tempted to stay all day.

*

Following an uneventful three-mile journey from Hallbridge back to Camley, the taxi deposited Lucy at Aunt Eleanor's small, semi-detached house. Most of the guests would have already been there an hour or so. Lucy had calculated 12:45 p.m. to be the latest polite arrival time possible.

"Hello," said Eleanor, looking resplendent in a green floral dress and clashing blue necklace. It wasn't joy unbound, although they air-kissed.

"Hello, Eleanor," said Lucy, hoping her yellow blouse over navy blue chinos would meet the dress code. "Lovely to see you."

"Is Richard coming?" Eleanor enquired, seemingly more interested in Lucy's brother.

"No, he texted to say he's snowed under at work."

"Oh... pity."

Lucy smiled. Eleanor had never had a job, although she often recounted a desire to join the diplomatic service as a young woman before seeing sense and getting married instead. World War Three averted, Lucy always felt.

In the cramped, over-furnished lounge, a dozen others had gathered. Greetings were exchanged while Eleanor disappeared into the kitchen.

Lucy took in the oil painting over the fireplace. It was Sir George Howard, looking like a 1920s hipster with his full, fuzzy beard. The one thing he had valued more than anything was the family's standing in the community, even as the progress of the 20th Century laid waste to tradition and decorum. As per his postcard from Monte Carlo in 1925, he reminded them, 'What does the ordinary person see when they behold a Howard? It's a question that must guide our every action.'

"Libby's in the loo," said a woman called Mo, who had been on the Camley scene since moving from 'noisy' Brighton twenty years ago.

Lucy nodded. She too would use the loo ploy at least twice over the coming hours.

"Libby and I spoke the other day," said another guest. "She's thinking of buying a new phone. Well, she's had her current one five years."

Lucy smiled. So, Libby had plans.

As suspected, Jane wasn't there yet. She was always busy. It was an even bet she wouldn't bother to leave her home in Littlehampton at all. And Lucy knew all about betting.

"How are things?" asked Mo, coming to join her.

"Not too bad, thanks. How about you?"

"Oh fine. Number one son is at Manchester doing his master's degree in Technology. Number two son is at Southampton doing History. Baby daughter is revising for her GCSEs. She wants to do History at A-level. It's a simply wonderful school, of course. The sixth form is the best in the area."

"Great," said Lucy, now remembering that Mo's life was only ever described through the activities of others. "How about you and Harvey?"

"We're fine. Harvey's doing something with the garden. There's a new shed and a bench area… it's all go. How about you? Any thoughts on settling down?"

"I already have. I've got a nice place in Barnet and a good job at a college in Hatfield. Easy for commuting as

I'm outward bound when everyone else is heading in."

"I meant relationship-wise."

"Ah, well, that's…" *none of your business…* "all fine, Mo. I'm not looking for a relationship. Life's too busy."

Lucy let her gaze wander in the hope of picking up on something distracting. While others guessed at the arrangements and timings that would get them through the celebrations, she settled on the family photographs that adorned the mantelpiece below Sir George's imperious gaze.

"Ooh photos," she said with feigned enthusiasm.

Among the twenty or so framed portraits going back over half a century was one of Eleanor's daughter, Jane, sitting astride an antique rocking horse.

Ned…

Ned had once belonged to Lucy's mum who had given the horse a name that stuck – even when he was passed down to Richard and Lucy, and on to their cousins. The memories were strong. Influenced by the Wild West movies her grandad, Tommy Holt, loved to watch on TV, seven-year-old Lucy would readily spend time on Ned, chasing after the bad guys and bringing them to justice.

She pulled up the cloud storage space on her phone.

'Photos' folder. Subfolder 'Childhood Photos'.

The contents of nine family albums had been scanned and uploaded – a seemingly unending process carried out during a college two-week Christmas shutdown.

Photo 0062: 'Lucy, age 7, on Ned, age 100+'.

While most photos recalled past times in a passive way, this one always grabbed her by the hand and hauled her back, so that she could feel it, smell it, almost touch it. She smiled, although not as keenly as the little girl looking back at her from forty years ago.

"Attention everyone!"

Eleanor was in the middle of the room brandishing a photo album.

Had Lucy's mother been alive, this would have been exactly the same. Just like her late sister, Eleanor took showing off the family's superiority to a professional level.

"Here's sixth-former Libby with Anthony Crosland, who came to the school."

Lucy smiled. *Who the heck's Anthony Crosland?*

But Eleanor wasn't finished. "Mr Crosland was, of course, Secretary of State for Education and a very good friend of the famous American politician Henry Kissinger."

"It's a lovely photo," said Mo, squinting at the small black and white snap, "but Libby's missing all the fun."

Eleanor ignored her.

"This one is Libby with Princess Anne at an outdoor sports event."

Again, Lucy smiled. *Hmm, speck-in-the-crowd Libby watching Princess Anne. Hardly 'with'...*

"And here's Libby with television personality Peter Glaze at a sixth form visit to the BBC in London."

Lucy's smiling was beginning to cause cheek-ache. Fortunately, being a reception desk veteran, she would cope.

"I haven't simply got these photographs out solely for Libby," said Eleanor. "I'm actually researching the family history for a book on the Howards and our influence on West Sussex from the end of the War to the end of the 1970s."

Lucy dropped the smile and donned her earnest look. Trust Eleanor to usurp her sister's party for a spot of self-promotion.

"It sounds great," said Mo.

"It hasn't attracted a publisher as yet," said Eleanor, "but the research continues."

"Ah Libby," said someone, and all turned to the party girl in the doorway.

*

The distribution of the cucumber sandwiches went like clockwork, accompanied by Eleanor's crushing analysis of the dreadful cucumber sandwiches served at a recent local summer fete. And, in between Eleanor's account of her current charity committee duties, kind words were spoken about Libby, describing a generous woman who always put other people first. Being a Howard girl, being a granddaughter of Sir George, being a charity fundraiser – these were the details that were celebrated.

"I recall a time," said Eleanor, "when Libby was determined to beat all-comers during the build-up to a charity jumble sale. She collected so much clothing to put into the sale that we could only see her head from behind the pile. She looked like a clothes monster."

Everyone laughed politely, including Lucy. So many good words had been spoken here over the years. She wondered if any of those sentiments had imbued themselves into the fabric of this place to elevate it above other people's lounges.

"And now, Libby," said Eleanor, stepping back.

Lucy relaxed. What did Libby have to say for herself? What kind of speech had she worked on?

Libby stepped forward, the pale blue cardigan over her floral blouse making her look stylish and yet overdressed for a warm day.

"Thank you for coming," she said with a welcoming smile. "It's so good to see you all. Do make sure you have a piece of cake."

Libby stepped back. The speech was over.

"Let's liven things up while I arrange teas and coffees," said Eleanor. She pressed a button on her ancient hi-fi and Lucy became aware of a low-volume rendition of Beethoven's Ode To Joy. That was fine. Eleanor wasn't likely to play 'Wonderwall' or 'Do Ya Think I'm Sexy'.

Making her way to the loo, Lucy unexpectedly decided that she would like to be buried in a forest. After a natural death, of course. Not murdered and buried as part of some foul enterprise. And buried deep. She didn't fancy a fox digging her up and running around with one of her legs in its jaws. She wasn't sure why that occurred to her.

In the pink tiled bathroom, she didn't need to go and so opened the window a little and peered out over the garden. Below, Mo was regaling someone with details of her sixteen-year-old baby daughter and a simply wonderful school…

Lucy knew the kind of school she meant. She had attended one herself. She always knew it was a top school because her parents reminded her almost daily. When Lucy's daughter Victoria joined a comprehensive school in Barnet, Lucy's mum had been dead a number of years, but there was always that ethereal sense of her not approving. Of course, Eleanor just came out with it. A comprehensive school? How dreadful.

The Howards…

A Monte Carlo postcard…

'What does the ordinary person see when they behold a Howard? It's a question that must guide our every action.'

Lucy checked her watch and left the smallest room. Another hour, she felt, and then she could bid them all farewell. She would use that hour to talk to Libby. After all, that was her reason for being there. It was with disappointment then that the first person she saw on re-entering the lounge was fresh arrival Jane Ranscombe, her cousin.

3

Jane

Jane...

Unsurprisingly, she was wearing a shirt and jeans – okay, so a stylish, off-white designer blouse and expensive-looking charcoal denims. Their eyes met, Lucy gave a faint nod and they smiled. It was good to get that over with. Maybe they wouldn't need to talk much beyond hello, nice to see you – as had been the case over the past thirty years on those few occasions where they had both attended the same gathering. Certainly, Lucy wasn't planning to position herself where Jane would remain out of direct view for the remainder of the party. Although, now that Jane had started taking selfies with people, a slight delay to engagement seemed a reasonable compromise.

Lucy stepped to her left to be with Mo, blocking out Jane with a least three people.

"They say it should be a nice weekend," she said, adopting a suitably sunny disposition.

"Yes, I might do a little tidying up in the garden while Harvey's busy with his shed," said Mo. "We all need a little sunshine, don't we? In fact, we're thinking of going to Greece next year. Have you ever been to Greece? It's very much Factor 50 sunscreen country, isn't it."

"Yes, absolutely," said Lucy. "The one time I went to Greece I got horribly burnt."

"Oh?"

"I used the highest factor protection, but I stupidly went to cool down in the sea on an inflatable dragon and it washed off. Not thinking, I carried on bobbing up and down for far too long and ended up with red raw shoulders. I had to get some special cream from a pharmacy."

"Nasty. Oh, I must speak to Henry…"

Mo wandered off to join another attendee.

"Hi, Lucy," said Jane, appearing almost out of nowhere with a glint in her eye.

"Hello, Jane." Lucy felt herself tensing up.

"We really should have a proper catch up."

For all the world, Lucy didn't want to spend a minute with her cousin, but she couldn't ignore the fact that if she could steer a safe course through the encounter, future sightings might drop down to a mere amber alert.

"Yes, a proper catch up would be great. I'm just about to talk with Oscar. I'll get back to you as soon as I can."

Lucy turned away to gatecrash a man called Oscar's talk with an unknown middle-aged woman about German right-wing extremism. Lucy nodded and studied their faces, and then, for a second time, studied the photos on the mantelpiece behind them.

Little Jane smiling astride Ned the rocking horse…

Eleanor unexpectedly joined them and was soon praising foreign students who came to British universities to work hard – unlike homegrown students who were, according to Eleanor, obsessed with s-e-extra.

Just then, Mo butted in.

"Lucy, that time you were bobbing up and down for so long it made you red raw, what cream did the pharmacy give you?"

Lucy couldn't get the words out. Neither could Eleanor, who looked somewhat perplexed.

Mo, spotting Eleanor's confusion, explained. "Lucy had protection, but it didn't work."

"Mo's talking about the time I went to Greece," said Lucy, but that didn't appear to help either. "Sunburn. I had burnt shoulders."

Eleanor took a breath and eyed Lucy. "My book will cover a number of fascinating areas. Your mother will be mentioned, of course, and I'd like you to let me have any amusing stories you know about her life before you were born. I'll sift through them to see what might go in."

Lucy noted that Oscar, Mo, and the unknown middle-aged woman were moving away. She smiled at Eleanor as best she could.

"I'll try."

"So, how's Victoria? Has she met anyone yet?"

"No, but she's happy house-sharing with three other young women and getting ever more involved in her job in animation."

"Animation…?"

"Yes, do you remember? I told you she decided not to go to university? She's been with a studio in West London for two years now."

"That's lovely. And how about you? How's work?"

"Oh, it's fine, thanks."

"It's admin duties, isn't it?"

"Yes, I might have mentioned it before?" *Like, a million times.* "I'm a reception manager and refreshment coordinator at a theological college."

"Refreshment coordinator?"

"We organize career break refreshment, sabbatical refreshment, spiritual refreshment…"

"It must be nice to be settled in a job. Jane's starting up another enterprise. She's already running the online children's partyware store and children's book business, servicing over a thousand parents, but you know our Jane. Next stop, children's toys. I'm sure she'll tell you all about it herself."

Lucy supposed toys would sit well with books and partyware.

"She's so lucky to be involved in things she has a knack for," she said.

"Hardly luck, Lucy. Jane works her socks off. She's sacrificed a lot."

"Same with me," said Lucy, wishing she wasn't saying it even as the words came out. "I mean in terms of loving what I do – not in terms of success."

"Loving what you do *is* success," said Eleanor.

"Yes, it is. I've always believed that. Otherwise, I'd walk out tomorrow."

"Ellie takes after her."

"Does she?" Ellie was Jane's twenty-year-old daughter, currently away at university in York. "You mean business-wise?"

"I was thinking more in attitude. Not giving a fig for what others think. Getting on with it. Never say die. But always with the highest standards. Last time I saw her, she told me she'd discovered the secret to a happy life."

Lucy raised an eyebrow. "Impressive for a twenty-year-old."

"She said she discovered it when she was thirteen but didn't like to sound precocious."

"Right, so what is this magical formula?"

"Stop making excuses and get on with it."

"Hmm, she does sound like her mum." But Lucy smiled. She was pleased for Ellie. And for Jane too. It was good to see people getting on with it. Lucky Jane and now lucky Ellie.

She wondered. Were some people born lucky? Yes, they worked hard but there was luck there too. Had she been blessed with luck herself, what would she have gone on to achieve? Joining the police force seemed a daft idea now. But it hadn't been daft back when she too was a precocious thirteen-year-old.

She looked around. Eleanor had been sucked into someone else's conversation, leaving Lucy free to think of taking a small sherry from the catering table.

Before she got there, she caught sight through the French windows of Aunt Libby alone in the garden.

Lucy stepped outside.

"Can I get you a drink, Libby?"

"I'm fine, Lucy. You carry on."

Libby gave that smile of hers – the noble one. Sensing something wasn't quite right, Lucy went to join her.

"Are you okay?"

"I'm fine."

"I see Eleanor's writing up the family history. I tried some research a while back on a genealogy site, but I got confused during the Victorian period. I must try again sometime."

"No need. Eleanor's sure to cover the Victorian era and first half of the twentieth century once she's finished with the post-War years. I'm sure she'll make copies available at a discount."

"The Howards... we had a genuine standing in the community."

"A wonderful reputation."

"You and Uncle Eddie certainly kept that up."

"That's very kind of you to say. He was the best, you know. He always gave his time to whatever cause. He was a real pillar of the business community. Everyone looked up to him. He was just unlucky to have that heart problem."

Lucy could picture him – a gin in one hand, a cigarette in the other, an aversion to walking anywhere or doing any form of exercise…

"Yes, he was a much-loved man," she said. There was no need to counter Libby elevating him to sainthood.

"Do you think you might let someone into your life again?" Libby asked.

Lucy was immediately on guard.

"I don't think so."

"It's been a while since James, hasn't it?"

"Yes…" *James the drunk, the gambler, the addict…* "ten years."

The coroner's report said he might have survived the crash just outside Camley had he not been in such poor physical health. But they say every cloud has a silver lining – and for Lucy, it was the opportunity to take a job eighty-five miles away in Hatfield and rent a place for herself and Victoria in Barnet. No more dodging Jane at school summer fetes and Christmas plays…

"What about you, Libby?" she asked. "Any plans? No romantic plans, obviously. Well, not obviously, but…"

"I know what you mean. No, there'll never be anyone after Eddie. I do have some plans though. Or rather, I did."

"Oh?"

"I had a lovely offer from a dear friend of mine. Do you know Gail Middleton?"

"No."

"She recently moved to a lovely little place on the coast at Selsey and suggested I move down there with her."

"You mean buy a house nearby?"

"No, pay to have her adjoining garage turned into a granny apartment."

"That sounds nice. What does Eleanor think?"

"Eleanor?"

"Obviously, it's none of her business, but…" *But she does rule West Sussex.*

Libby shook her head. "Eleanor leads a busy life. All those committees she's on. I'm on none of them. I'm very supportive though. I'm always making small financial contributions to her causes."

"Of course – so Selsey?"

"Yes, well, as of yesterday, it's on permanent hold."

"Oh, that's a shame. What happened yesterday?"

"I had a little setback. You see, I have an antique silver cup…"

Jane stepped outside – a glass of sherry in one hand, her phone raised in the other. She took a photo of Lucy and Libby and then came to join them.

"Hi, guys. Avoiding me?"

"No, of course not," said Libby. "I really must pop to the loo though."

Lucy was annoyed. Something serious had happened to Libby and here was Jane trampling all over it.

"You *have* been avoiding me though," said Jane.

"No," said Lucy, her eyes fixed on Libby going back inside. "There have been various people to talk to, that's all."

"I mean you've been avoiding me for a number of years. Too many to count, really."

A small bird flitted by. A great tit or a coal tit? And

now Jane's phone was looming above her as her cousin moved alongside for a selfie.

Lucy supposed the one thing that defined Jane was her oneness. What you saw went all the way through. Succinct. Forthright. It went from the sweat on her brow to the DNA in her bone marrow. Lucy feared her own duality of cheery exterior, fearful interior would always make this kind of encounter difficult because it required two trains of thought.

"Perhaps this isn't the time to bring up the past," she suggested cheerfully, her gaze settling on her cousin.

"Those were strange days, weren't they?"

"I barely remember any of it," said Lucy, upping the cheeriness factor. "Thank God we've all moved on."

"I'm sorry I missed your dad's funeral. I was already on my way to Italy."

Lucy smiled understandingly.

"How's Simon?" she asked, referring to Jane's younger brother.

"He's fine. Divorced and working in London. How's Richard?"

"He and Sophie are both well and very busy. They won't be coming."

"Oh."

"I'm impressed by your mum writing a book. That's quite a task."

Jane laughed. "She's not writing a book. She's talking about it, at length, to anyone who'll listen."

"It sounded like she's doing a lot of research into the past."

"She doesn't have to research the past. She lives there. I sometimes think this whole family lives there."

"It's a proud family," said Lucy. "We... well, *they* have always done good things in the community. I know it's a bit old-fashioned these days, but I'm proud of them."

"Fair enough. We both grew up with family members being on charity committees and parish councils. It's all come to an end now though. We have to go back to Eddie for anyone doing anything that anyone paid attention to."

Lucy didn't like Jane's dismissive appraisal, and yet it was hard to challenge her.

Jane took a sip of her sherry and smiled. "Do you think that's why Libby married him?"

"He was a good man. I remember him being on some important local enterprise committees."

"Do you reckon he got Libby all steamed up with his sexy business talk?"

"That's not funny."

But Jane seemed amused by it. "Oh darling, I've invested five hundred in a tech start-up."

"There's no need to be crude."

"You and me – we were absolute best friends. We would have died for each other. What happened?"

"It's all in the past. Let's leave it there."

"Seriously?"

"Yes, seriously."

Jane sighed. "Whatever you think, Lucy, I never ruined your life. You did that all by yourself."

4

Old Haunts

A couple of hours after the party, Lucy was back at her hotel in Hallbridge thinking about Libby. A subsequent chat had failed to stir anything relating to her obviously miserable situation or the mysterious mention of an antique silver cup. Libby had decided to shut the matter down. Something was wrong though.

Questions formed. Should she see Libby prior to heading home in the morning? Or would a phone call suffice? That was Lucy's usual approach when it came to family matters.

Her phone rang. It was her daughter.

"Hello, Victoria. Is everything okay?"

"All okay, Mum. How did it go? Have fun?"

"It was fine. We all got together to celebrate a good life well lived."

"You make it sound like a memorial service. I thought Libby was full of *joie de vivre*?"

"She is – usually."

"She looked great in the photos. Hasn't aged at all!"

"What photos?"

"Ellie's mum shared them online and then Ellie shared them."

"I didn't know you were in a group with Ellie?"

"Mum, we were at junior school together."

"Of course…"

Victoria and Ellie had spent three years together at school in Camley – not that it ever brought Lucy and Jane into contact at the school gates. Lucy had an admin job in Chichester in those days and relied on Libby to take Victoria to school and bring her home.

"Are you going through with your plan?" Victoria asked.

"Yes, I think so."

"You think so? You seemed really up for it when we spoke."

"As I recall, you were pushing me, but yes, I'm going in a minute."

"Good. Don't forget to take some selfies."

"Yes, about that…"

"It's okay, I know you don't like sharing online. We'll have a glass of wine and a laugh over them next time I'm over."

"Right, well, I'll say bye-bye and get to it then. I'll report back when I get home."

"Okay then. Bye, Mum, I love you."

"I love you too."

Of course, her daughter didn't get it. Not fully. That was Lucy's fault. All that endless recounting of her happy early years had long become a way of counteracting the late teen years, of which Victoria had heard nothing.

So, unremarkably, a routine chat a few days earlier had brought up good memories. Pre-seventeen memories. But talking to her daughter over coffee, Lucy experienced a sudden realization of how disconnected she had become from those far-off days, as if they had been placed behind a screen. So maybe Victoria hadn't needed to push much after all.

She checked her watch. It was another two hours before dinner. So, as planned, she left the hotel on foot. It was only a short walk to the past.

*

Shelby Avenue was a non-descript street. The kind that told you nothing. In fact, the kind that suggested there wasn't anything to tell in the first place and that nothing had happened since it was built in 1932.

The semi-detached houses were all similar, set back from the road with a short drive and a strip of grass. The fences between were generally covered by mature shrubs or well-maintained privet hedges. Little had changed since her teenage years. Little ever changed in Sussex. It was a county that exuded permanence.

A pizza delivery bike came crawling along and pulled up opposite. The familiar sight of the rider taking hot food to someone's door.

Lucy headed down the street – nearing the house the Robertsons lived in all those years ago. She paused where Mr Robertson's little red Ford once sat on the drive. Now, the grass was gone and a Range Rover, a Mercedes, and a sporty BMW took up the entire block-paved front.

A little farther on, Lucy crossed the street and came to a halt outside the Pendletons' place. Here, Steven Pendleton once kissed her and suggested they might like to get married. Then he invited her to try on his Batman outfit. Him being five and her six at the time did not diminish the strength of the memory.

Finally, outside number 23, she stopped with greater

purpose. There was her mum at the lounge window... and behind her a small girl on a rocking horse. Her dad, Eric, appeared at the door – a tall-ish man in a business suit that matched his job as an accountant, or as Mum used to put it, a wealth consultant.

"Can I help?"

The image of her father dissolved into a man in jogging attire. The new people who had taken over. She had never met them personally and didn't wish to.

"Sorry, wrong number," she said.

She walked on a little way, aware of him leaving the house and pounding away in the opposite direction. A moment later, she took out her phone and pretended to talk to someone as she walked back on the opposite side to take in number 23 from neutral territory.

Her mum had died aged forty-seven – the same age as Lucy now. Her dad would have been fifty-four at the time.

Relationships are risky. Her parents' marriage failed. It was only her dad's good grace that kept them together. But it hurt Lucy to know they had separate bedrooms seven years before her mum fell ill.

Her dad stayed on in the house for another quarter of a century, living there quite alone until his passing. She wondered about that for a moment. Then she heeded her daughter's suggestion. It seemed the most ridiculous thing, but she turned around, raised her phone, and snapped herself in front of her old house.

So many memories...

The first time she took a boy up to her room. Sixteen. Homework. Supposedly. Not that much of their planned snogging could take place. Her mum constantly interrupted with tea, lemonade, biscuits, magazines...

That was when Lucy first began to fully understand

the extent of her parents' difficulty with people displaying passion. She certainly couldn't remember them ever displaying any themselves. She recalled playing at a friend's house when she was six or seven. The friend's dad came home from work and kissed his wife right there in the lounge where Lucy and her friend were playing. Just like that! Lucy was shocked. Her head swirled. How did they know it was okay to kiss? They never spoke a word!

She thought of her mum again. A Howard girl. She had occasionally displayed emotion, of course, but she tended to save it for arguments – or, more accurately, for the end of an argument, where she would storm out of the room and slam the door shut as an exclamation. Lucy had long hated people slamming doors. It always triggered anxiety.

She wondered. What was it with relationships? Why were they so hard to get right? She had let three men into her life. All of them lost causes – lost causes she had believed she could turn around, rescue from the brink, restore to the light, possibly because she was a Howard, and helping the less fortunate was a valued family trait. She recalled Jane introducing her to Greg, saying he needed a bit of help, and would Lucy like to get involved?

Bad memories.

Lucy sighed. Coming here had been a mistake. She should have gone home to Barnet straight after the party.

She turned back in the direction of the hotel and started walking swiftly along the streets of her youth. It brought back more memories. Hurrying, late for school…

She slowed. The past didn't own her. She just wanted to revisit happy times. Why was that so difficult?

She reached the main road. Up ahead… the White Horse pub. She recalled being allowed inside at seventeen, mainly because back then nobody ever asked for proof of age, and possibly because the landlord knew her parents.

Yes, the White Horse, which, along with the Prince Regent, served this large-ish village as well as a few smaller communities nearby.

She couldn't help but glance across the street as she passed on the opposite side. Maybe they had redecorated it, reshaped it, smashed the old interior into rubble and rebuilt it leaving just the exterior façade. She wouldn't be going in to check. For her, it would remain as it had been that evening, when she set foot inside and beheld tall, handsome Greg alongside sixteen-year-old Jane waving to her from the bar.

*

Later, back at the hotel, Lucy mulled over her choices while she enjoyed the in-house grilled halibut and mashed potato, which helped dissipate the effects of Eleanor's terrible cucumber sandwiches and weak, watery coffee.

She wouldn't be visiting her old junior school on the other side of the village in the morning. The charm of the idea had simply worn off. And as for visiting her old high school in Camley...?

While it was easy to skip over the bad bits from afar, here on the little-changed streets of West Sussex, she was all too aware of what she was avoiding. Like the time she was in sixth form and Greg came by on a motorbike – obviously stolen, although at the time she had gullibly believed it to be on loan from a friend.

No, this had to stop. Sussex had to be returned to the past, to memory, and she would have to stop telling Victoria how lovely certain bits had been. From now on, she needed to act like a grown-up. She would tell her daughter everything or nothing. And nothing seemed the better option, because frankly Victoria had lived through enough bad stuff herself, with a drunk, gambling father hardly ever there for the first ten years of her life, and then permanently gone when he crashed his car.

One advantage of not going to take selfies outside her old haunts in the morning would be having some time to spare before she headed home. Something wasn't quite right with Libby and she didn't want to leave Eleanor or Jane to deal with it. Not that they would have even noticed.

Later, around half-ten, she got ready for bed. Beyond the hotel window lurked a dark Sussex sky. She once dreamed of such nights, with someone who loved her, who made her laugh, who would hold her close.

She checked her phone. No messages and nothing out of the ordinary on Facebook. She checked the selfie she had taken earlier. A middle-aged Lucy Holt looked completely out of place outside teenage Lucy Holt's home.

She slid under the covers and closed her eyes. Sussex offered nothing. In the morning, she would check on Libby and then go straight home to Barnet.

5

The Silver Chalice

On a lovely early September morning in Camley, having paid the taxi driver, Lucy paused with her wheelie bag at Libby's front gate.

It was a moment to take in a view that had captured the spirit of sunny days going back at least the twenty-five years Libby had lived there, and very likely many years more. The clematis that climbed either side of the high gloss royal blue front door was in bloom, its cheery yellow flowers basking in sunshine. Quite simply, the old stone cottage was quintessentially charming. It was also ideally located for anyone responding to a summons from Eleanor, a few hundred yards across the town.

The front door opened.

"You really didn't need to come," said Libby. "You'll miss your train."

Lucy smiled. "Don't worry about the train. It's an hourly service. As long as I avoid the Friday afternoon rush hour in London…"

Inside, Libby unnecessarily recounted the latest UK weather report while she prepared a pot of tea and a small plate of chocolate fingers. Lucy was aware that the country could expect a few days of warmer weather, but she hadn't come to talk about meteorological conditions.

However, Libby was already in full swing, extolling the joys of sunny days generally and then homing in on memories of sweltering trips to Bognor, Brighton, and the horse racing at Goodwood. It was a while before they made it into the lounge with the tea and biscuits.

"I was worried about your little problem," Lucy explained as they took their seats. "You were very vague yesterday, but I sensed something was troubling you more than you were letting on."

"You mean Selsey?"

"Yes. What's going on?"

Libby pondered for a moment before answering.

"It's not like I won't see her. It's not that far."

Lucy still didn't get it.

"What was the plan? You mentioned a granny apartment."

"As I explained, my friend Gail Middleton recently moved there and thought I might like to join her. It would mean me paying for her garage to be turned into a living area with a separate bedroom and *en-suite* bathroom. We had a couple of quotes to do the conversion work and it comes in at around thirty thousand. Obviously, I'd have a stake in the freehold based on a valuation."

"So, what's changed?"

"I don't have the money."

"Right… so why did you get quotes for the work?"

"Because I thought I *did* have the money. That silver cup I mentioned – it's an Elizabethan communion chalice that dates back to 1580."

"Wow. That's old."

"Yes, Eddie obtained it years ago. The thing is… the

man at Taylor's Antiques in the High Street believes it only dates back to the early twentieth century. Pre-First World War, probably."

"You mean it's a fake?"

"He used the term 'copy'."

"I see."

"He said an original would be worth around twenty thousand."

"Again, wow."

"He offered me five hundred for it."

"Five hundred? I hope you told him which lake to jump into."

"It's alright, I'm just working up the courage to try another dealer. It was quite a blow hearing what he had to say."

"Just make sure you don't sell it to him."

"No, I wouldn't. It's worth a lot to me sentimentally. Obviously, that would change for twenty thousand. Eddie would have wanted me to be happy. He wouldn't have wanted me to part with it for five hundred though. He would have had something to say about that."

"I'm glad, but... I mean, it's none of my business, but couldn't you sell your house and buy a house near your friend?"

Libby looked around her, at the walls, the door, the ceiling.

"No, that wouldn't be possible."

"Oh... any particular reason?"

"I don't own it."

"You don't? Oh, I always thought..."

"It's a rented property."

"Okay. I suppose I'd always assumed... still, no matter. There's nothing wrong with renting. I rent. So did Dad."

"Except, you can only move if you find another place to rent."

"And there aren't any?"

"On the contrary, there are quite a few. It's just that I'm seventy and I wouldn't feel comfortable trusting my peace of mind to a new landlord. You read all kinds of rotten stories in the newspapers, don't you. Mine does every little job and even sends a gardener round twice a month at no extra cost."

"I don't suppose your friend could contribute to the cost of converting the garage?"

"She lives on a small pension. She owns the house, but really has little else. I couldn't possibly ask her to pay even part of it."

A glaring solution reared up in Lucy's mind.

"Have you thought of asking Eleanor for a loan?"

"Eleanor? I couldn't ask Eleanor for money. Goodness, the world would freeze over. Chasms would open and consume southern England. At least that's how bad it would feel should I ask. No, Eleanor and I never discuss money. Absolutely not. It's out of the question. Besides, Eleanor wouldn't believe my financial situation. Apart from the house, she thinks I have a portfolio of shares and a considerable sum in the bank."

"And you don't?"

"No."

Good grief.

"So why does Eleanor think that?"

"Because I've always given her that impression. Believe me, having Eleanor's pity would be unbearable."

"The pity is that you and your sister don't have a more honest relationship."

"I'm desperate, Lucy. I'm so disappointed I can't go and live with Gail. I'd do anything to change it."

"Right..."

"I have two thousand in the bank for a rainy day and there are other bits and pieces I could sell. Raising thirty thousand with the chalice was going to be tough, but without it..."

"Fair enough," said Lucy, trying to fathom how successful businessman Uncle Eddie had left Libby with next to nothing.

"I'll be fine," said Libby, gathering her emotions but failing to fully hold them in. "You know what it's like to have life-changing plans... to reach a moment of exciting transformation..."

"Yes, of course." Lucy experienced a sudden urge to change the subject. She opted for Libby's son. "I meant to ask – how's Keith getting on?"

"Oh, he's well. He moved to a new school last year – on the outskirts of Sydney. He loves being part of the senior management team, shaping the way the school runs."

"Australia sounds wonderful. His partner's a teacher too, isn't she?"

"Kimmy? Yes. They met at his first school over there. That's fifteen years ago. How time flies."

"You went over to see them not so long ago, didn't you?"

"Yes, that would be nine years ago."

"Nine?"

"We do the video thing on the phone a couple of times a month. It's not the same as being there though."

Libby became lost in thought for a moment before pointing to one of the photos on the wall by the fireplace.

"Do you remember him like that?"

It was young Keith astride Ned the rocking horse.

"Funny you should say that. I was looking at photos

with Jane and me sitting on Ned. Separately, I mean. I expect you passed old Ned on a long time ago."

"I meant to, but I never got around to it."

"You mean he's still here?"

"Would you like to say hello?"

Lucy felt a pang. A bubbling up of feelings that echoed from happy days long ago. She could already sense his white painted body and horsehair mane and tail.

"Come on," said Libby.

A moment later, they were in the garage pulling the dust cover off.

Lucy gasped. "Oh Ned…"

She felt a kind of joy that was all too rare in the world. At least, in her world. Warmth radiated throughout her body, her being, her soul.

"He's as lovely as I recall," she said, studying him… her oldest friend… forever in full gallop.

"He probably needs a good scrub with detergent," said Libby.

"He looks fine – although not quite as big as I remember."

"Well, you've grown. For the record, he's still four feet high from the floor to the tips of his ears."

"To think Mum had him when she was young."

"We all did," said Libby. "After Sylvia, he was passed to Eleanor, and then to me. Then, when your mum had you, she took him back for you. Eventually, he ended up back here for Keith."

"I'm glad you kept him."

"Ah well, there wasn't anyone to pass him along to after Keith. It's only recently I've thought of selling him. No room at Selsey, you see. That's why I know his dimensions. I was going to write an advert."

"We were crime-fighters," said Lucy, stroking Ned's

mane. "We used to chase after the bad guys."

"That sounds fun."

Lucy wanted to say how she carried the notion forward with schoolgirl ideas of becoming a police officer. But that would only lead to talk of Greg and of being arrested, which she and Libby had spent thirty years pretending never happened.

"Wonderful days," Lucy said instead. "We never think we're going to grow up. Everything is in front of us."

"Lucy... our tea's getting cold."

"Yes, of course."

A few moments later, in the lounge, tea in hand, Lucy wondered how to broach a tricky subject.

"Please don't take this the wrong way, but Uncle Eddie was a successful businessman."

"Let's not talk of sad times, Lucy."

"No, but I was wondering how someone as experienced as Eddie could get so badly caught out by a fake antique." She knew not to suggest that Eddie might have been a fool.

"Eddie was a good man," said Libby with evident pride. "I was so lucky to have met him."

Lucy, having not been quite so lucky in meeting Greg, James, and Leo, wanted to get to the bottom of it before she caught a train back to London.

"Do you really think the chalice is worth twenty thousand?"

"Honestly? I have no idea. We never had it valued."

"Not even for insurance purposes?"

"It was never insured."

"Seriously?" To Lucy, something didn't ring true.

"Eddie said it would be too expensive," said Libby.

"So, you just took a chance that it would stay safe?"

"We hid it in the loft between the joists under the

water tank."

"Well… that sounds safe enough."

"It'll have to go back up there soon. Would you like to see it?"

"I'd love to."

Libby took a quick trip up to her bedroom and back. In her hands was a beautiful silver cup the size of a coffee mug, along with a separate lid. It lacked the kind of extravagant engravings Lucy had been expecting. The only decoration was a band of leaves going around the cup, with a similar design around the edge of the lid. She supposed the plainness matched the period in which it was made – or at least the period it was faking.

"May I?" she asked.

Libby handed it over. Just like her silver vase at home, it was cold to the touch, and yet it had the warmest charm.

"It's lovely, Libby. How can the dealer tell it's a copy?"

"I'm afraid I can't recall his exact words. I was in a state of shock."

"You poor thing…"

Lucy was getting a deepening sense of things not being at all right. What if the chalice were genuine? What if the dealer hoped Libby's deflated self-esteem would induce a capitulation? What if he got back in touch next week with a revised offer? Say, a thousand?

No, she couldn't get involved. She had her own life to lead. Libby had just run into some bad luck.

Welcome to the club.

Lucy suppressed the feeling that this needed fixing. Yes, she wanted to see fair play – it was her standard response to any unjust situation – but she was learning to dispel such urges for the sake of a saner life.

"You must try another dealer," she said.

"I probably will," said Libby, "although, I get the feeling it's a bit of a lost cause."

"Think, Libby," said Lucy, despite the need to maintain her non-involvement. "Did he give you *any* details about what was wrong with it?"

"Well... now I think of it... he might have said something about the markings on the bottom."

Lucy studied the markings and tried to apply some logic to the situation.

"I don't suppose there's much point in trying another dealer without fully understanding what the problem is."

"Indeed," said Libby.

Lucy bit her lip. She really didn't want to get dragged into this. But Libby looked helpless. And hopeless.

Lucy checked her watch. "Would you like me to pop round there before I head home?"

"Oh, would you? I'd be ever so grateful. I was thinking of asking but it's so embarrassing. He made me feel like a crook."

"Right," said Lucy, feeling a rising need to chase after the bad guys. "Let me take some photos of it."

It was 9.45 a.m. The hope was to resolve things quickly and catch the 11:22 London train. With a bit of luck, she would be back home by half-two to give her kitchen a good clean and polish in time for the weekend.

6
Taylor's Antiques

In Camley's picture-postcard High Street, Lucy paused outside the Georgian façade of Taylor's Antiques, with its *olde worlde* bay window and doorway. The building had to be two hundred years old, she guessed. She didn't recall there being an antiques place here. Then again, ten years had passed since she lived in the area.

Preparing to enter, she felt a little anxious about challenging an expert over her aunt's chalice, but accepted that sometimes, you simply had to do what you could to help.

She pushed the door open. Fittingly, an ancient tinkly bell rang above her head as she stepped into a world of quiet. Of gravity. Of ages.

Beyond the antiques on display, right at the back, a middle-aged man was speaking quietly on the phone. Mr Taylor, she presumed. He was at his 'desk' – an informal setup of a laptop on an old dark wood bureau and a couple of Regency chairs, one for him and one for the customer, although he was alone right now.

She liked the way he dressed: smart-casual with a

lightweight tan jacket over an air-force blue shirt – possibly silk. He looked across and smiled. It made her feel warm. Obviously, he smiled at everyone. It was part of the job.

From her vantage point, she took in the various aspects of Taylor's.

Against the side walls, left and right, the larger objects stood. A range of cabinets, dressers, and a grandfather clock.

Down the middle of the room, from the front door to the back, a line of varied tables hosted small pieces such as carriage clocks, candelabra, weighing scales, a letter rack, a small telescope, and more.

Open display cabinets at the back housed the more breakable items, such as vases, cups, and plates.

Near the proprietor's desk, small, valuable items, such as watches, rings, medals, and many silver items were in closed glass cabinets.

And finally, all the wall space above the displays was covered with framed paintings.

The grandfather clock chimed ten. It was the sound of the 1880s. Sherlock Holmes might have checked his pocket watch against it.

Lucy turned her attention to a small, elegant, highly polished desk by the door. The label declared it to be a Victorian mahogany writing table. It was priced at £775.

She ran her hand over its surface. The wood was cold to the touch, as was the green leather inlaid part. She could smell the sheer age of the thing.

"You like that?"

It was the man, no longer on the phone. He was heading straight for her, his smile coming ever closer.

"I was thinking how elegant it is," she said.

"It certainly is. Would you like to know more?"

He was right in front of her.

"Please."

"It's Victorian, around 1860, possibly a little later. As you noted yourself, an elegant piece – mahogany with a leather writing surface. It's in good original condition with bags of character and charm. Nicely turned legs, too. You could get one at auction for five hundred, but not in this condition."

Lucy slid open one of the two drawers. It wasn't mahogany or leather she could smell. It was sandalwood. As in aftershave.

She looked up to him.

"I'm Lucy Holt. I'm actually here on behalf of my aunt."

"Oh, Nick Taylor – welcome to my little place. Is your aunt looking for a writing desk?"

"No, she came to see you about a silver communion chalice. You gave her a valuation."

"Ah, that sounds like the lady who came in a couple of days ago. Has she decided to sell it?"

"Ha!"

Lucy immediately tried to withdraw the 'ha', but such exclamations are strictly one-way.

"Ha?" The smile had gone and the frown that replaced it wasn't at all welcoming.

"I'm sorry," said Lucy. "I don't usually do outbursts. You took me by surprise. I'm not being rude, but offering an elderly lady five hundred for an item that could be worth twenty thousand is… well…"

The dealer's frown deepened. "An original Elizabethan sterling silver communion set, circa 1580, might be worth twenty thousand. A 1910 reproduction is strictly in the hundreds. And I didn't offer to buy it. I suggested she go away and think about it. I also suggested she get a second opinion. If, on reflection, she was happy to take five hundred, I suggested she might come back."

"I see."

"Has she had someone else value it?"

"Not yet. She's still a little shaken."

He noticeably softened. "I'm sorry to hear it, but this sort of thing goes on all the time. Fakes, copies, reproductions, homages…"

Lucy felt the fight leaving her. This man was the custodian of a genuine and wondrous emporium.

Even so, she tried to regain her zest for the job in hand by accessing the photos she had taken with her phone.

"It looks genuine," she insisted, showing him the item in question.

"Absolutely, it does. Good fakes often do."

Lucy flicked to the next photo.

"It has hallmarks."

"Yes, but they're not genuine."

Lucy tried the next photo, which showed the hallmarks in close-up.

"They look original."

"If this were an original piece, I'd telling you it's an exceptional two-piece set consisting of a chalice and paten…"

"Paten?"

"That's the circular pedestal foot. You place the cup on it. You can also turn it over and use it as a cover, a lid…"

"Ah."

"It has fine patination – that's the level of tarnish you'd expect – and, understandably, it's rare. Often, the paten is missing."

"How can you tell it's a copy?" Lucy asked, tucking

her phone into her coat pocket.

"Okay, those hallmarks… they're too softly struck. Do you understand hallmarks?"

"No."

"Okay, so the marks tell us the maker, the purity and so on. But they're fake. It really isn't any more complicated than that."

"You're not trying to trick a respected elderly lady?"

"You think I'm a conman? You certainly know how to make an impression."

"No, I'm not saying that at all."

"Then you're suggesting I don't know what I'm talking about."

"No, of course not. I'm just trying to do the right thing for my aunt. Only, I have no idea what the right thing is."

The dealer sighed. "As I recall, she said it was her late husband who obtained the cup. Maybe you could find out how he came to own it."

"Unfortunately, I don't have the time. I just thought… well… it doesn't matter. I'm sorry to have questioned you without having the facts."

The dealer's phone rang. He checked the display.

"Sorry, I need to take this," he said, moving away for privacy.

Lucy believed him. This was a wonderful assortment of antiques and it was highly unlikely he was a conman. Not that she was an expert at spotting character flaws – at least not until it was too late.

What could she do to help Libby? She was hoping to catch a train in just over an hour.

"Are you waiting for Nick?"

Lucy looked across the vista of antiques to a door at the back. A woman of around seventy had appeared.

"I'm not sure. I think our business is probably done."

"I couldn't help overhearing – I was polishing some pieces out the back. I'm Fay."

"Hello, I'm Lucy."

Fay came closer. "I saw the chalice your aunt brought in. It's such a lovely piece, but if Nick says the marks aren't right then that's it, I'm afraid."

"Yes, well, tell him not to worry. I won't be calling the police."

"He'll be pleased. The local inspector isn't his friend."

"Oh?" Lucy's suspicion bristled.

"Detective Inspector Crawford's wife bought a fake painting for two thousand from a fake dealer operating out of an office in Arundel. He made himself known at a couple of auctions, made promises, made money and then – pwoof – made himself disappear."

Lucy liked Fay. How old was she...? Probably not far off the age Lucy's mum would have been, had she lived.

"A fake painting," Lucy mused. "How was Nick involved?"

It felt odd using his name.

"He was the bearer of bad news," said Fay. "He did an insurance valuation, estimating the inspector's wife's investment to be worth fifty pounds. Ten minutes later, Inspector Crawford had half the county force on the case."

"Nick's not a con artist then."

"No."

"And his offer to my aunt was genuine."

"For the record, he said he'd be happy to buy it should she wish to sell it, but, as always, he insisted she get a second opinion."

"It's standard procedure," said Nick, heading back having finished his call.

"Well, thanks for your help," said Lucy.

"If you're not in a hurry, I could show you some examples of hallmarks," said Nick.

"No, really, it's fine. Thanks."

"Okay then."

He offered his hand. She shook it. He had a nice firm but friendly grip. And he was smiling again, which she preferred to the frown.

"No other questions?" he asked.

Something wonderful and worrying struck her. Nick's hair was a little ruffled, his eyes friendly, his smile, nice, his voice, engaging, and his waistline, a little full, suggesting he wasn't a gym obsessive. He seemed at ease with the world.

"My aunt had a bit of bad luck, that's all. It happens to the best of us. Thanks again."

She nodded to Nick and Fay and left Taylor's Antiques.

She was disappointed. Not at leaving Nick behind – anything else would have been ridiculous. But it might have been interesting to get involved in a mystery. Although, there probably was no mystery. The facts, as always, would most likely be mundane. Smart, super-duper Uncle Eddie had brought home a dud. Years after the event, and with Eddie dead, what would be the point in trying to find out exactly how stupid he had been?

7

Going After The Bad Guys?

The ten-minute walk back to Libby's gave Lucy some time to get her thoughts in order. She would explain to her aunt that, unfortunately, Eddie had been duped. She would sugar-coat the pill by explaining how the antiques dealer, Nick, believed the chalice to be a top-notch reproduction capable of fooling quite a few experts. She would then advise Libby to display it, enjoy it, and let it remind her of happy times with Eddie.

There was something about Nick though. Not the question of honesty, but her enjoyment of their brief close proximity. At work, there was a middle-aged man called Tony who often came into close proximity. She never enjoyed that.

Jane once asked if she believed in love at first sight. They must have been twelve at the time, and Jane followed it up by bursting into a fit of giggles over a boy at school.

Forty-seven-year-old Lucy mused on it. Setting aside love at first sight, she suspected that attraction at first sight was as old as Time. There was no denying the pull she had felt. But a pull to what? Excitement and fun? Or yet another opportunity to make a fool of herself?

*

Back at Libby's, Lucy recounted Nick's thoughts on the matter – making sure to protect Eddie's reputation as a wise man. For a moment, she imagined his gravelly smoker's voice. "Have some adventures before you're too old, girls." He was talking in that gin-soaked way some people do – waving their drink around in a cavalier fashion yet never spilling a drop.

"Do you think he's honest?" Libby asked.

"Who, Nick? Yes, I do. He seems very genuine and, as he says, you really ought to consider getting another opinion."

Libby somehow looked older than her seventy years. The weight of this thing was clearly heavier than she was letting on. She retrieved the chalice with its lid on and placed it in Lucy's hands.

"What do *you* think?"

Lucy felt its weight, its quality. She studied the markings stamped into it. And then she set it down, with the lid turned over to provide a base on which to stand the cup.

"Oh, is that the right way round?" Libby asked.

"Either way is right."

Lucy could only wonder how this simple object could make such a difference to someone's life.

"Sorry, Libby. Apart from having a few collectibles and watching the Antiques Roadshow, I know absolutely nothing about this kind of thing."

Libby sighed. "I suppose we'll have to put it down to bad luck."

"Yes..." But Nick's words came back, even though Lucy didn't want them to. "The only alternative is to look into where Eddie got it."

"That was years ago," said Libby. "He said he took it as payment for services provided."

"Do you know who he was working for?"

"No, sorry. He always had at least three things going on at any one time and I really didn't get to know more than a fraction of his associates. I think his problem was his benevolence. And I mean that in a good way. He probably trusted someone he shouldn't have, but I wouldn't change a single memory. He was a wonderful man."

"Yes, he was."

Lucy knew all about wonderful men. She had let three of them into her life. Only, having entered as wonderful, they each departed as somewhat less than wonderful. She briefly thought of Nick, but that wouldn't be going anywhere, whether he was wonderful or not. His smile though... a little like Leo's. But then the seven thousand pounds she lost came to mind.

"Can you recall *any* of them?" Lucy asked, forcing her thoughts back to the matter in hand.

"Eddie's associates? He was very much a phone man. Back in the eighties, he was the first person in Camley with one of those big portable phones. I can see him now, pacing up and down in the garden with that oversized thing pressed to his ear. That's how he liked to do business."

"Right, so there's no one from those days who sticks in your memory?"

"The only person I can think of who knew him well is Jason Hall. You know St Luke's Church?"

"Yes, of course. Is he on the staff there?"

"No, Jason runs a pawnbroker's opposite. He and Eddie were friends going back to their school days. They played golf most Saturday mornings."

"It's worth a try, I suppose," said Lucy, doubtful that this could ever be resolved.

"Oh, thank you, Lucy. It's very kind of you to offer."

"No, I mean *you* should follow it up. I don't know him from Adam."

"Jason's place isn't far from the station. I find it so embarrassing…"

"I can't ask a money lender about a fake antique."

"No… no, I suppose not. I'm sorry, I probably watch too many detective shows."

Lucy smiled sympathetically. "We're all guilty of that."

Twenty minutes later, she was waving farewell.

"Keep well, Libby."

"You too."

Lucy walked off down the street, pulling her wheelie bag behind her.

She thought of Libby – sad and alone. Then she pulled out her phone. A quick text to her daughter to say that all was well.

But was all well?

She opened the phone's photo gallery and found a specific photo.

Ned…

She chewed on her bottom lip. How time changes us, she thought. How events bear down on our progress. A little girl on a wooden horse. Seven-year-old Lucy and Victorian Ned. The purity of the thing. That was it. They never got bogged down or sidetracked with neuroses and doubt. They never troubled themselves with what others might think. They never considered the possibility of failure or embarrassment. They simply went after the bad guys.

*

Pawnbrokers. Money lenders. To Lucy, they were a cliché. Not in real life, but in TV dramas. That's where they lived in the consciousness of those who never required their services. On TV, they always performed the same function – to provide moral clarity at a crisis point in someone's life. Things would be going badly, a cherished item would have to be hocked, the stakes would be high for the character…

In real life, she supposed people handed over their trinkets in exchange for money to pay the rent, and then reclaimed the items when they got paid or received their state benefits. Hardly a drama worthy of TV, but still tragic, she felt.

Up ahead, a sign pointed to the station.

She could see the church coming into view. What was the right thing to do? Not just for Libby, but also for herself.

No, not for herself, but for seven-year-old Lucy… and for seventeen-year-old Lucy…

Didn't she owe them something?

How did Greg describe her to that detective inspector all those years ago? A stupid piece of posh trash? An easy ride? An over-privileged airhead who liked hanging around bad men? He got word to her later that it was his way of protecting her from prosecution. The police would look upon her with pity. But she had wanted to become a police officer. She didn't want his statement read out in court describing her in that way. She didn't want her parents and Aunts Libby and Eleanor in the public gallery wincing and looking mortified. She didn't want it quoted in the local newspaper. But whereas people in her family's past had wielded power, she did not. And when she let them all down, she shamed the Howard name and threw away her future.

But what of now? Had she become the person who leaves a desperate old auntie to her fate? Was that a self-image she could live with? Or, as usual., would she bury it and tell Victoria of a lovely visit to sunny Sussex?

A few moments later, Lucy entered Jason Hall's premises trying to affect an air of 'I'm not a customer' and realized this was exactly how a Howard girl should act. However, the two actual customers being served at the counter failed to notice her arrival.

"Is Mr Hall here?" she asked the young woman behind the security glass attending to them.

"That's me," said a voice behind a bead curtain in a doorway behind the young woman.

He emerged holding a mug of coffee and indicated that Lucy should join him at the other end of the counter. Being a schoolmate of Eddie's meant Jason had to be in his seventies. If anything, he looked older.

"How can I help?" he asked.

Lucy was quite happy for him to be behind glass. He had an unseemly air about him.

"I wonder if you could help me on behalf of Libby Cole. She's the widow of Eddie Cole, an old friend of yours."

"And you are?"

"Lucy Holt, Eddie and Libby's niece. I work for St Katherine's Theological College in Hertfordshire."

She had no idea why she had told him where she worked. He was hardly likely to say he knew of it or that he understood they offered a very good refreshment package.

"So…?"

"Right, so, I'm trying to find someone who might be able to help with a little mystery concerning Eddie."

"We were friends going back to our school days. What's the mystery?"

His face gave nothing away, leading Lucy to assume he must be good at poker – another thing learned from TV dramas.

"Aunt Libby had a silver chalice valued recently. It was something Eddie received in lieu of payment for services rendered." Lucy lowered her voice. "Libby believed it to be worth twenty thousand pounds. The antiques dealer valued it at five hundred. He said it wasn't an original piece."

"I see," said Jason, in an equally low voice. "That's bad luck."

"Do you recall Eddie mentioning a silver chalice? Libby said you were golf partners. Maybe he mentioned something while you were out on the fairway."

"You make it sound like one of those TV detective shows," Jason said in a much louder voice, which Lucy took as a dismissal of the subject. "I don't recall Eddie talking about antique silver of any kind. Mind you, he kept his business activities to himself – which is something we can all learn from."

"Right… well… I suppose it was a bit of a long shot. Poor Aunt Libby. She's in a right state. Eddie must be looking down from above worrying about her."

She gave Jason her saddest smile.

He sighed. "Eddie used to work with a bloke called Francis Randolph."

"A business associate?"

"Yes, although for business purposes most people know him as Fast Frankie."

"Fast Frankie?"

"I believe he still hangs out at a snooker hall in Brighton."

"Right…" But while Lucy's head was nodding, her thoughts were churning.

I represent a theological college. I can't meet someone called Fast Frankie at a snooker hall.

"Yes, Fast Frankie," Jason repeated. "I wouldn't lend him any money, if I were you."

Lucy jotted down the details, thanked him, and left.

She was soon back on track for the station thinking that Fast Frankie sounded like a character from a 1950s B-movie. Not that she could pursue it. At least, not without help. And she certainly couldn't ask Nick to assist. That would lead her into areas she wasn't ever going back into. She had tried to help Libby – that was the main thing. And, at the bottom of it all, getting involved in other people's lives never ended well.

Greg flashed through her thoughts again. On that occasion, she went from upstanding young citizen to despised low-life vermin in two chaotic months.

She dismissed it. On this occasion, she had done her bit and could return to normality.

Satisfied, she opened her phone's photo gallery with the intention of deleting those shots of the silver chalice. However, facing her was the photo of a little girl on a wooden horse, looking set to go after the bad guys.

8

Train of Thought

Aboard the 11:22 to London, clutching a milky coffee purchased a few minutes earlier from the station café, Lucy felt drained of substance. The photo of her eager young self, sitting astride Ned, ready for action, had brought on a heavy dose of self-loathing.

She took a careful sip of her coffee and considered her existence. Was it predictable and dull? No, of course not. She led a full life, had a good job, and she was a useful member of society. Why rock the boat?

She thought back to Greg, the criminal lost cause, to James, the gambling and alcohol lost cause, and to Leo the dating conman who, for a time, seemed everything she needed in life – so much so that she dropped all her barriers. Her blood ran cold.

Her phone rang. It was Libby.

Odd...

"Libby? Is everything alright?"

"I've decided to pursue the matter."

"I'm not quite with you."

"I wracked my brain and recalled Alan Wilson. He was

a semi-retired antiques dealer in the 1990s. Only, he was already in his eighties then."

Right, so now he's the oldest man in the world.

"Libby…"

"He might have written a diary or something."

"That's quite a long shot. I don't think you should be following that up."

"No, I suppose not."

But Lucy could feel Libby's hopelessness. The chances of finding out what happened were slim. But Libby was desperate to move to Selsey, and Lucy could not walk away. Except she was. And not walking but riding at fifty miles an hour.

She imagined being at work. Happy in her non-eventful routine. Booking an archdeacon into three days of refreshment. And all the while, Libby's plans would be ash.

"Look, when I'm back home I'll make a couple of phone calls."

"Who to?"

"I'll google Alan Wilson and see what comes up."

"Thank you. I know it's not your field but thank you."

"Leave it with me. I'll be in touch."

She ended the call and stared out at the lush trackside foliage zipping by the window. Alan Wilson. There should only be about two million of them on Google.

She made a call to a number she had recently noted. There had to be a route to the truth.

"Hello, Nick? It's Lucy Holt, the silver chalice enquirer."

"Hi."

"I just spoke to my aunt."

"Okay."

"I just wanted to say that she understands and accepts

that you've acted professionally. She never intended to suggest otherwise. I think it was the shock."

"Of course. No problem at all. Tell her I'm sorry I couldn't give her better news."

"She mentioned Alan Wilson, a dealer back in the nineties."

"Okay, if he's still active, I should be able to find out where he's trading."

"No, he'd be 110 by now. It was more if you'd heard of any doubts regarding his reputation."

"You mean if he was a crook?"

"No. Well, yes. I mean I don't know. My poor aunt is taking it really badly. I just... well, you know."

"Of course. I wouldn't hold out much hope though."

Lucy decided to push a little.

"You're right, of course, but... well, this is a bit hypothetical, but what would you do if Libby were *your* old auntie?"

"*My* old auntie?"

"Yes, who would you see? What questions would you ask?"

"Look, I'm sympathetic, but there's nothing I can do. Libby's husband was the only one who knew what happened and he's dead."

Lucy couldn't argue. Nick was right. It was a lost cause. What's more, these would be the last words she spoke with him, which seemed a bit of a lost opportunity.

"Thanks for being so understanding, Nick. You've been patient, helpful and polite."

"You're welcome. Unfortunately, there's no shortage of fake silver."

"I just wish I could help my aunt. I'm due back home though. Work calls."

This was ridiculous. She didn't want the call to end.

There was an intimacy that was all too rare in her life. Of course, he was merely being professional.

"What is it you do?" he asked.

"Oh… I'm a reception manager and refreshment coordinator at a theological college."

"Refreshment coordinator? You mean you organize the coffee and croissants?"

"You know as well as I do a refreshment coordinator organizes career break refreshment. Sabbatical refreshment. Spiritual refreshment. We run courses."

"Oh, *that* kind of refreshment."

"It's perfectly normal in a theological college setting."

"Well, there you have the advantage. I take my refreshment in the pub. Tell me, does the team wear T-shirts with a big 'R' on the front?"

"What team?"

"Team Refreshment."

Lucy wondered – maybe she was wrong about Nick.

"It's a much-loved course. People come from all over Europe to stay with us."

"I'm sorry. I was teasing and that's not fair. We don't even know each other. I'll let you go now."

"Yes…"

Lucy had a rare moment of emotional clarity. She was as certain as the bongs of Big Ben that she did not want Nick to go. There wasn't time to analyze it. She just knew she had to act.

"Before you go, Nick…"

Before you go – what??

"Yes?"

"Well, speaking of… you know…"

"Um…?"

"I was just wondering…" *What?* "…are you a good judge of people?"

Why am I asking him that?

"I suppose so. You have to use a bit of instinct in the antiques trade. We really do meet all sorts. How about you? Would you say you're a good judge of people?"

"Me?" Leo flashed through her mind. Leo, who she met online seven months ago. Leo, who used the next three months to sweet-talk her out of £7,000. "Yes, I'm a good judge of people."

"I had a feeling you might be."

"You get to meet all sorts at a reception desk."

"I'm sure you do," he said with a hint of mirth. "Well, I ought to let you go."

She didn't want him to go. She was enjoying his company. But what could she say that wouldn't sound idiotic?

"Nick, what do you know about antiques?"

"Er…?"

Okay, ludicrous question.

"Sorry, I mean, to be specific…" *What??* "………antique… rocking horses!" *Yes!* "Victorian, to be exact."

"I'm no expert, but there were some leading horse-makers back in the day. I'm trying to recall the names… Lines, Collinson, Ayres. A fully restored Victorian horse could set you back five thousand."

"Wow, that's a lot of money. It's just that my aunt has one."

Even as she said it, Lucy realized she didn't like the idea of Ned being sold to a stranger. Maybe she could buy him herself. Not for five thousand though. That would require a bank loan. Although, she doubted Ned was in tip-top condition. Would Libby take three? Or would that make Lucy a hustler?

"Why don't you pop in next time you're passing?" said

Nick. "We could discuss rocking horses over coffee and cake."

Oh.

It all came crashing into her brain. The silver chalice, Ned, Libby, Nick. And she was hurtling away from them all on a sparsely populated train.

She calmed herself. This was the end of a short trip to Sussex for Libby's birthday. Heading home was by far the sanest option. A good life awaited her back home. Having alternatives swirling around in her head didn't make an iota of sense.

"Lucy?"

"Can I get back to you?"

"Of course."

She ended the call feeling certain that ways of life couldn't simply be tossed aside. If choices were made there would be consequences. She couldn't get involved with Nick. And, besides, he wasn't suggesting any such thing. He mentioned coffee and cake, not a wild fling.

The train began to slow. They were pulling into a station. She was still a long way from London, but if she were to act on Libby's behalf, and get to the bottom of it all, she would need to start right away. It was either that or stay on board, forget the whole thing, and get back to an uncomplicated existence in Barnet and Hatfield.

9

There's a Man Called Francis

Lucy hauled her wheelie travel bag out of the station and paused to look up at the sky. Would it rain? The weather was meant to be good. Maybe it was just a passing cloud. In the concrete canyons of Central London, it was easy to survive without thinking of the weather. That's why she preferred living in the northern suburbs and working farther afield in Hertfordshire.

That closer connection to the natural world applied here in Camley too. And she was glad for that.

She phoned the Prince Regent Inn in Hallbridge, deciding that, at least for now, she would maintain a three-mile distance between herself, Nick and Libby.

Yes, they had a vacancy. Would she like her old room again? They made it sound like a home from home. Maybe it would become just that, depending on how long she planned to stay. Of course, she had no idea. She just told them to leave it open-ended for now and that she would talk to them later.

Yes, she was about to make a fool of herself, but what the heck. An old horse called Ned had called her back.

Trundling up to the High Street, she wondered what Nick would see in her. A plucky individual? Or a meddlesome sticky-beak? It was hard to know.

What if she were Jane? Then what?

Jane, obviously, would ask Nick out to dinner. No fuss, no lack of confidence. He would say yes or no and she would cope ably with whichever answer she got. It wasn't the same when people had punctured your reserves of self-confidence time and time again. Still, it wouldn't hurt to be bright and breezy – in much the way she greeted visitors to St Katherine's.

She thought of Victoria saying, "Mum, you're cut out for more than a theological college's reception desk." Her daughter saw it as the ultimate comfort zone. She was probably right. Certainly, there was never any stress. Well, maybe that time an archdeacon noisily broke wind while he signed in. But they just pretended it never happened. She had explained to Victoria many times that, comfort zone or not, it was nice to work in such a civilized ecosystem.

She reached Taylor's Antiques and took a breath.

Here goes…

But, on the verge of pushing the door, she noticed a handwritten card stuck to the inside of the glass: 'Back in 5 mins.'

Great.

She consoled herself. At least the sun had come out again.

While she waited, she thought of texting Victoria to say she would be staying on for a bit longer. But what would she type? 'I hope to persuade a man to help me look into a mystery surrounding a fake antique'…?

She would never send such a text, of course. Victoria knew all about Leo. Their texts would quickly become an argument. And who would be right? The sensible daughter or the mother who had exchanged words of love via a webcam with a conman who stole most of her savings?

Sometimes, usually in bed around midnight, Lucy feared she might be stuck in an endless cycle of failure. The trusting fool. The gullible victim.

She shook it off and texted Victoria that she was staying on to help Libby with one or two things.

Having done so, for some reason, she thought of Aunt Eleanor once describing how the War generation had coped so wonderfully. Men switched from office clerk to soldier blowing up enemy positions and then back to office clerk. Likewise, women raised children on powdered egg and hopeful news reports.

Stress? Never!

Her phone pinged. It was a text from Jane.

'Hi, Lucy. An apology. I didn't mean those words. Sorry. Could we meet up to clear the air. Not just from yesterday, but from the past thirty years. I can come up to London. Would that work for you?'

It took a moment for Lucy to decide. Then she typed:

'I'm still in Sussex.'

Almost immediately, a text came back. Not from Jane, from Victoria.

'You and Libby live a little xx.'

"Hello again."

Lucy looked up. It was Nick's assistant, Fay, coming along the street.

"Hello, Fay. I was wondering where Nick might be?"

Fay pointed up the street.

"A hundred yards on the right. Bingham's Auctioneers. He's looking over the latest arrivals."

"Oh…"

"He should be back soon. Fancy a cup of tea?"

"Oh lovely, thank you."

Inside, over tea and biscuits at Nick's desk, Lucy relaxed a little. Fay seemed to have a calming effect.

They discussed a number of topics, including the weather, the 150th anniversary of St Luke's Church, the recent air balloon festival, and the price of electric cars. It was a good ten minutes before Fay brought them to something more salient.

"I'm guessing that chalice is interfering with your plans."

"Yes, it is a bit, but it's fine. I suppose Nick must face this kind of thing every day."

"Buying and selling antiques has its traps, but Nick knows what he's doing."

"How long have you been with him?"

"Ten years. I worked here for the previous owner when it was a wine store."

Lucy seemed to recall it as such. Yes, now she thought of it, she had definitely bought a few bottles of cabernet sauvignon here. She didn't recall Fay though.

"I offered to give Nick a hand for a few days," Fay continued, "just until he settled in. I knew absolutely nothing about antiques."

"But you do now."

"Well, perhaps a little."

"I love antiques in an Antiques Roadshow kind of way," Lucy admitted. "The stories are always fascinating."

"Every antique has a story to tell," said Fay. "We just rarely get to hear it."

"That's what my grandad used to say," said Lucy, thinking fondly of her father's father, long-gone Tommy Holt.

"Well, your aunt's cup has a story, I'm sure. It's no

surprise that someone should try their luck making a copy. Silver is incredibly popular. It ages well and people tend to look after it, so there's a lot of good stuff around."

"I suppose people have enjoyed showing it off down the centuries."

"Probably, but centuries ago, there was a functional reason for using silver cups and plates. Unlike cheap pewter, it resists bacterial growth, so the wealthy wouldn't fall ill."

Just then, a customer came in.

"Hello, I'm looking for a clock for a mantlepiece."

Lucy thanked Fay and left her to it.

"Bingham's Auctioneers," Fay called after her.

Lucy and her wheelie bag were soon trundling down the street, although the nearer she got to Bingham's, the more she began to feel she might be imposing on Nick. Or possibly even constituting a nuisance.

At the entrance, she peered in through the glass doors. The interior appeared to be full of old furniture but devoid of people. Perhaps they were only open to the trade.

She suppressed her doubts and pushed on through. She immediately spotted Nick's head above the furniture on the far side of the large room. She waved, which felt a bit strange, especially as he hadn't seen her come in. She continued waving a little more animatedly. Still he didn't see her. She felt a fool, but that was nothing new.

Just then, another dealer noticed her and worked out what was going on. He called to Nick, who looked first to this man, and then in the direction of his pointing finger.

He smiled and came over.

"Lucy?" He eyed her wheelie bag. "What's going on?"

She explained the situation regarding her aunt and

how it would be wrong to abandon her.

"So how can I help?" he asked.

"Yes, good question. The thing is… there's a man."

"Okay."

She couldn't bring herself to say 'Fast Frankie'. It was too preposterous.

"His name is Francis Randolph. Would you be able to use your contacts to see if that name comes up?"

"Yes, of course, but I'm really busy at the moment. Could it wait?"

Her heart sank. This wasn't going to be quick.

"Do you have a database?" she asked. "I'm good at calling people and getting details."

"My database, as you call it, is strictly confidential. Sorry."

"Of course." She was at a loss. What was her next move?

"Would it be possible to leave it with you, Nick?"

He glanced at her bag.

"Sorry, leave what with me?"

"The search for Francis Randolph."

"Ah, look, we seem to be at cross-purposes. I haven't got time to phone around in search of missing persons. My list is hundreds long."

"Right. Just a thought – couldn't you put all your contacts on an email list? Then you could send out a single email to all of them. That's what I do."

Nick seemed unimpressed.

"Lucy… I provide a bespoke service for clients and I'm always respectful of fellow professionals. I do not send out block emails."

"Right. Yes. Well, I'd better be going then. If you do get a chance to contact them one at a time, it's Francis Randolph. Also known as Fast Frankie."

Nick's face changed again. It seemed to be mimicking that time she tried a banana and mayo sandwich.

"Okay… who exactly is this Frankie character?"

"Libby's husband Eddie used to work with him. I think he was a kind of business associate. He hangs out at a snooker hall in Brighton."

Nick was looking even more puzzled. "And who told you all this?"

"A pawnbroker called Jason Hall."

"Right… okay… and this is everything he told you, is it?"

"He also said don't lend Frankie any money."

Nick sighed. "Okay, look, I know a man. He's… well, he's not on my official list. He's what you might call a bit questionable. He might know something. No promises, mind."

"No, of course not. Is he based nearby?"

"He tends to hang out at unofficial venues. You know, round the back, off the beaten track, kind of thing. There's always one coming up somewhere in the south of England. You just have to know where and when."

"And to think you're friendly with Detective Inspector Crawford."

"Hardly friendly. Although I do now advise his wife on antique purchases. Leave this with me. I'll get back to you as soon as I can. Leave your details with Fay."

"Okay, thank you. That's very kind."

"We'll have that coffee and cake when we get a moment."

"Yes, I'd like that."

Lucy left Nick to his search for antique treasure.

Outside, she decided to give Fay her phone numbers, both personal and work, and then get over to the hotel. Hauling a wheelie bag around was becoming a chore.

Just then, her phone rang. It was her cousin.

"Hello, Jane. Is everything alright?"

"Lucy… this is going to sound a bit odd, but would you be able to help me with something? It's Aunt Libby. She's roped me in to find out the story behind a fake antique. Crazy, right?"

"I don't understand."

"It's that silver cup she showed you."

"No, I don't understand why she asked you. I told her I'd deal with it."

"Oh right. Awkward."

"Awkward? Why?"

"She assumed you wouldn't see it through."

That stung, but Lucy did her best to ignore it. "So, she asked you."

"Yes, but I'll need help if I'm going to take it as far as I can in a day or two."

Lucy waited for the hurt to subside. Fate, for some horrible reason, had turned back the clock. Her cousin was once again taking over. Libby had weighed the situation and decided who could and couldn't be trusted to get things done, to see it through, to make a difference.

"Lucy?"

"Yes, of course I'll help. It's for Aunt Libby. When would you like to meet?"

10

The Junior Partner

Lucy was at Eleanor's, waiting in the lounge for Jane to arrive. Not that she was deep in conversation with her aunt – Eleanor was on the phone in the other room organizing a military campaign, or possibly a coffee morning. Lucy felt that here was another missed opportunity for utilizing mass email.

Ignoring the twenty or so family photographs that adorned the mantelpiece, she checked the clock that sat in the middle of them.

1:02 p.m.

Jane was meant to be there at one. Of course, the clock might have been wrong, but that seemed unlikely. It sat below an oil painting of Sir George and belonged to Eleanor. It wouldn't dare.

Lucy huffed. She was still a little raw from being cast as a slacker by Libby. She was keen to help, but to be Number Two to Jane was going to take a degree of fortitude. It would be like the time she was Assistant Reception Manager at the college when her boss, Liz, retired. Instead of promoting Lucy, they put Tim from

Events in as temporary cover. It was a form of purgatory only relieved when Tim became too busy with an international conference and asked if she could take over for a few days. Lucy did so, changing everything as quickly as possible. When he came back and couldn't find or do anything without asking her, he gave up and returned to Events. She had been in place as Reception Manager for six years now.

She checked the clock again.

1:03 p.m.

The main thing would be to forget the silver chalice investigation hierarchy. This would be all about helping Libby – and Lucy would do so with decorum.

Eleanor appeared. "Sorry about that. Committee business. Would you like some lunch? I have plenty of cucumber left over."

"No thanks. Jane's taking me out to lunch."

"So… what's this about? You two hardly ever speak, now you're up to something. I can tell."

"It's nothing. We're just trying to help Libby with a little problem."

"Is it something I can help with?"

"It's to do with her finances."

"Oh?"

"She's been planning a move to the coast, but it's come to a halt. I can't say too much as it's her business, not mine."

"I see. Well, of course, she would never share her woes with me. God knows, I'm always here to listen. I can't think why she would want to leave Camley."

"No… but her best friend moved to Selsey recently."

"Selsey? You see, she has no sense. The taxi fares back here to see me will soon mount up."

"Yes… anyway… would you lend her some money?"

Eleanor's eyes widened. "That's not something we can discuss. As you say, Libby's affairs are her own. I'm sorry she's dragged you into whatever mess she's in."

"Our role is to do with an antique silver chalice she owns. Do you know the one I mean?"

"No, I can't say I do."

"Well, again, this is Libby's business and it's up to her whether she wants to tell you about it or not, but…"

"But?"

"Only to say she has an antique communion chalice she thought might be worth quite a bit, but it's turned out to be a fake."

"I see. What's the difference in value?"

"You should speak to Libby."

"No, I don't think so. That woman has never had much sense when it comes to money."

"It was Eddie who brought the chalice home."

"Eddie, Libby… I'd rather not get involved."

"Just for the record, Libby isn't desperate. It's just that Jane and I thought we might be able to help. You know, find out where it came from and why it isn't genuine."

"Well, you're in good hands. Jane is very able."

Eleanor's phone rang and she hurried off to answer it.

Lucy sighed. So, Jane was very able and, according to Libby, more likely to get things done. Lucy supposed she had no right to expect better treatment. She simply had no track record of venturing into the wider world and doing anything.

She studied the family photographs again, her gaze soon settling on young Jane sitting astride Ned. She wondered – did Jane ever pretend she was going after the bad guys?

She opened her phone's gallery and targeted Photo 0062: 'Lucy, age 7, on Ned, age 100+'.

The freedom, the possibilities, the hope…

She gazed at her young self.

I won't let you down. I promise.

Eleanor reappeared. "Scam caller. My BT broadband is about to be cut off. I'm not with BT, but they would never call to say that."

Lucy smiled. It was good that the older generation were becoming more resilient to fraud. She ignored the flash of Leo, who raced through her thoughts with a giant wad of her cash.

"I was just looking at Jane on Ned," she said, indicating the photo.

"Ned?" Eleanor squinted at the photo. "Yes, it was a lovely old thing, wasn't it."

It? Ned is not an it.

"Are you sure you have time for all this?" Eleanor asked. "I thought you were needed back at work."

"It's for Libby, so yes, I have time."

Eleanor shrugged. "You're right, of course. And I suppose it might be fun spending a week or two searching for clues."

"A week or two?"

Wheels began turning in Lucy's head.

"Or do you think you might conclude everything quickly?" said Eleanor.

The front door opened.

It was Jane.

*

Jane took Lucy to the Camley Kitchen for lunch. It was a vibrant local restaurant that did great food, although, judging by the background music, it was run by members of the Abba fan club. That was no problem for Lucy, though – she liked the band to the point of being tempted to sing along.

She wouldn't, of course.

The cousins were seated by the large bay window enjoying great toasted cheese ciabatta sandwiches with a generous side salad and glasses of iced water.

"Shame it's not prosecco," said Jane, eyeing her drink.

"Mmm," said Lucy, wholly disagreeing as that would mean the rest of the day being written off. James, Lucy's deceased husband, would have taken Jane up on it though. He would have written off two or three days.

"So, how's business?" Lucy asked. "Books, partyware and toys, isn't it?"

"It's going well. I'm waiting on deliveries across the board at the moment, so I have some downtime."

"It sounds ideal."

"One of my customers asked if I was doing it for profit or because I miss Ellie being young. There's something in it. Ellie's a young woman now but you never forget those days."

"That's what makes you successful."

"They grow up fast, don't they."

"Yes, they do."

"Still, it gives us our freedom back, right?"

Lucy nodded, but freedom was a funny thing. Jane was divorced from Lawrence and so probably felt liberated. Lucy was alone but couldn't say it was freedom she felt.

While they munched through their sandwiches and salads, Lucy wondered about Nick. He had yet to get back to her regarding his dubious source. She even checked her phone a couple of times but there were no texts or missed calls.

She held back on telling Jane about Francis Randolph. She wanted to see which way her cousin would lead the investigation. Very likely, it would be a less ridiculous route than going to a snooker hall in Brighton to pursue someone who did business as Fast Frankie.

"So, we're going to solve a mystery," said Jane. "It's like one of those TV shows."

"It's not," said Lucy. "Not really."

"What's that one with the two women… Cabbage and Parsnips?"

"We're just helping Libby, that's all. It's barely a mystery worthy of the word. She and Eddie were unlucky to get caught out and we're unlikely to get to the bottom of it."

"Cabbage and Parsnips would never say that."

"We'll do our best, but we can't perform miracles."

"It's funny though – I can't imagine Eddie and Libby hiding a twenty-grand antique in the loft."

"They couldn't afford the insurance."

"Yes, but why not sell it and buy a copy you could display in the lounge?"

"It was an investment for a rainy day."

"Maybe," said Jane, musing. "We don't know much about the real Eddie though, do we. We only have the 'pillar of the community' mantra to go by. What a cliché that is."

"Your mum's a pillar of the community."

"Exactly. All the Howards are, and so are those who are allowed to marry into the family."

Lucy bristled slightly. "There's nothing wrong with being an upstanding person in an upstanding family," she said.

"I don't hate the family," said Jane. "I just don't like the way it's made certain people lazy by giving them a sense of entitlement. For me, life's about questioning, challenging, doing. We should be building our reputations on our efforts, not have one based on an ancestor's standing."

"Yes… you're not wrong."

A silence ensued. It lasted a little too long.

"Getting back to smart Eddie…" Jane eventually said, "…how come he got caught out?"

"It's a good copy. He wasn't to know."

"I'm not saying he should have spotted it was a dud. I'm saying a smart person being given a twenty-grand cup in lieu of cash might have had it professionally valued."

Lucy thought about that for a moment.

"There are two possibilities," she said. "Either Eddie wasn't so smart, or he knew it was a fake. The thing is… if he knew it was a copy worth a few hundred, why hide it in the loft?"

"We need some info on Eddie's associates back then. Basically, who gave him the dud as payment?"

Lucy nodded and checked her phone. Still no contact from Nick.

"What do you think we should do?" she asked.

Jane puffed out her cheeks.

"No idea."

Lucy wasn't impressed.

"We're Howards," said Jane. "We should know what to do."

"You're a Ranscombe. I'm a Holt," Lucy pointed out.

"True. We've been watered down."

They spent the rest of their lunch talking about neutral topics – TV, the weather, globalization. Only after Jane had paid the bill and they were nursing the last of their water, did they touch on their shared history.

"It wasn't all rosy when we were young," said Jane.

"We certainly had a lot to live up to," said Lucy. "When it came to upholding family values, my mum was worse than yours."

"You're right there. Some days my mum would drive me absolutely nuts, but I could always console myself that at least I didn't have to live with cranky Aunt Sylvia."

Lucy found it strange when people referred to her parents as Aunt Sylvia and Uncle Eric. It made them sound like strangers. She supposed Jane felt the same way about her parents being called Aunt Eleanor and Uncle Jonathan.

"Uncle Jonathan's a good man," Lucy considered aloud.

"Don't say it – a regular pillar, blah, blah, blah. For the record, he and Mum had a miserable marriage. Yes, he ran a successful catering business and was a deputy mayor, but he was as cold as frost. In fairness, he's mellowed with age and a second wife."

Lucy put her glass down. This was getting them nowhere.

"Perhaps we should focus on Eddie's past," she said. "I don't want to spend weeks on this. We need to make a few enquiries and report back to Libby. I'm not hopeful but I'm keen to get started."

"Fair enough."

"So, what's the plan?"

Jane shrugged. "Not sure. I thought we'd try some antiques places in the area. Show them a photo of the chalice. See if it jogs any memories."

Lucy wasn't impressed. "Don't you think we should go after one of Eddie's old business associates?"

"Like who?"

Here we go.

Lucy stood up from her chair.

"How about we try Fast Frankie at a snooker hall in Brighton?"

"What?"
"I've got an address. Come on."
Jane frowned as she got up.
"Lucy, nobody's been called Fast Frankie since 1962."
But Lucy was already heading for the door.

11

Brighton

Their journey to Brighton in Jane's small, red Fiat began with a surprise.

"Did I mention I saw Greg?" said Jane.

Lucy's stomach tightened. She hated it when someone boldly, invasively, suddenly pronounced things like 'I saw Greg' or 'I've reached a decision about your job' or 'I have the results of your scan.'

"Oh?" she managed.

"He works for one of the supermarkets. Delivering groceries."

"They allow that?"

"How do you mean?"

"He has a criminal record."

"You think he might steal the bananas?"

"No, I just wondered. I suppose it was thirty years ago."

"He looked well."

"Oh. Did he suggest anything?"

"What, like a meet-up? He did, actually."

"What did you say?"

"I agreed to have a weekend away with him."

"Really?"

"No, of course not. I told him my husband wouldn't like it."

"But you're divorced."

"Lucy, what is the matter with you? Why do you have to be so literal?"

But Lucy's brain was always muddled when it came to memories of Greg. Of course, back then, she had simply responded to a call for help. It just so happened to have ended with her being sick each night with cold sweat dread of pregnancy and prosecution. The relief when she wasn't charged by the police. The relief when she wasn't pregnant. The plummet in self-esteem. The end of hope. Lucy saved Jane from trouble by covering up her involvement. And Jane flourished.

*

At the end of a sunny half-hour drive during which Lucy shared what little she knew about Uncle Eddie, Jason Hall and Francis Randolph, the two cousins were cruising out of Hove into Brighton. To their left, the grand Regency façade of Brunswick Terrace; to their right, the silver sea. They were soon passing the wreckage of the West Pier and Lucy was looking forward to seeing the Palace Pier. They turned off before they reached it though in order to find a parking spot. It was a further ten-minute walk before they were approaching their destination in the heart of the town.

"Lots of innuendo with snooker," said Jane.

"None of which we need to go into," said Lucy.

"I had a boyfriend who loved snooker smut in the bedroom. A firm grip on his cue. Endless references to balls. You get the idea."

"I'm assuming you weren't together long."

"No."

The snooker hall was above a pub, with a separate entrance at the top of a rusting iron staircase bolted to the side of the building. A sign on the door advised: Members Only.

Jane pushed it open.

Their eyes took a moment to adjust to the dark interior. Even then, it was still quite gloomy. The exception was a bright fluorescent strip-light over one of the six tables where a game was taking place. Beyond it, in the far corner, three men were seated at a small, round table playing cards.

Lucy looked around. There didn't seem to be a reception desk.

"Excuse me," Jane called out, not particularly targeting anyone. "We're looking for Francis Randolph."

Her enquiry was met with silence and blank stares.

"Frankie Randolph?" she added. "Or maybe Fast Frankie?"

More blank stares.

Lucy had an idea. Maybe Francis Randolph had more than one nickname.

Randolph… Randolph…

"He could be Randy," she ventured.

"Lots of men are randy, love," said a card player.

The others laughed.

"This is a respectable establishment," said one of the snooker players with faux indignation.

"We were sent by Jason Hall," said Lucy, pretending she couldn't hear their mockery. "He's friends with Francis."

But it was hopeless.

A moment later, back outside at the bottom of the iron staircase, Jane huffed.

"That went well."

Lucy was wondering what to do next when the door at the top of the stairs opened. A man in his fifties peered down at them.

"What kind of place does Jason run?"

"Pardon?" said Jane.

"I said what kind of place does Jason run?"

"A pawnbroker's," said Lucy.

"What's the name of the building opposite?"

"St Luke's Church."

The man nodded slowly, as if considering it.

"You don't look like police," he said.

"We're not," said Lucy, wishing she could say they were.

"There's an auction starting at four. It might be worth your while."

*

Lucy and Jane were strolling along the promenade overlooking the beach just west of the Palace Pier. They had around forty minutes to kill before the off-grid auction was due to start at the address the snooker club member had given them.

Lucy had doubts though. She was beginning to sense that they weren't moving forward with Libby's chalice but becoming sucked into some kind of semi-criminal cesspit. Eleanor felt it might take a week or two to get results and, so far, nothing suggested she was wrong. Libby's birthday – the real reason for coming to Sussex – seemed a long time ago.

"Do you remember coming to Brighton when we were

kids?" said Jane.

"Yes, I do. Our parents usually drove, but I remember one time we came by train…"

Jane broke into a smile.

"Did we misbehave?"

"Not *we*, Jane. You. You were rude about a couple."

"I remember! You said the man wanted to grope the woman."

"No, that's what you told our parents. You broadcast it to the entire carriage."

"Oh… so I did. And you got the blame."

"Yes, I got the blame."

Jane stopped to face the sea, seemingly lost in thought. Lucy stopped beside her. There weren't too many people on the beach. The busy summer season was over, and most families were back at work and school.

"You must miss them," Jane eventually said.

"I can see them now… down there in deckchairs… Dad smoking, Mum reading a magazine…"

"Yeah… I can see that too."

A thought occurred to Lucy. "Do you keep in touch with your dad?"

"I go to see him once a month. It's hard to believe he's eighty."

"Where does he live?"

"Near Southampton. He and Eve are pretty active. They'll go out for a meal or take in a show. And they have two weeks in Spain every April and October."

"That's nice to hear. I'm glad."

Jonathan's second wife, Eve, sounded perfect for him. Eleanor had never been one for restaurants or shows or travel.

"Do you remember buying fish and chips hereabouts?" said Jane. "It was that time our parents were trying to agree on a suitable restaurant for lunch."

"Yes, while they were discussing it, we nipped off to that shack and came back giggling and stuffing our faces from paper wrappers."

For Lucy, it was a warm, funny childhood memory. Although, now she thought of it, she did get into trouble for encouraging Jane. The perpetual price of being six months older.

"We were best buddies," said Jane.

"Yes, we were."

Lucy recalled their youth again. She was fourteen, Jane thirteen. Jane had a boyfriend who she made sure she kissed in front of Lucy. Lucy recalled the dread. The sickness in the pit of her stomach. The destabilization. At that point, their friendship was weakening with each kiss. While Jane was attempting to engage with adulthood, Lucy clung to the comfort of childhood. The boy wasn't even worthy — especially those times he guzzled cola and attempted to burp louder than a foghorn. You never got that in a Jane Austin novel. The horrible tension was only dispelled when, a few weeks later, the cola-burp boy kissed Lucy, meaning she could be a grown-up too.

"Lucy... I'm hoping we can be friends again."

"That's all I've ever wanted — for us to be friends. If I could turn back the clock..."

"I probably owe you money. You were always bailing me out."

"You led a busy social life. Even though we were at school."

"Ah school... do you remember that trip to the Natural History Museum?"

Lucy broke into a smile. The school trip to London was a fond memory. She and Jane practically laughed their way through the entire day, enjoying the many displays, but also cementing their friendship.

"I remember us straining not to giggle at Mr Trent creeping off every half hour for a cigarette," she said.

Jane laughed. "*Old* Mr Trent… loose in the Natural History Museum."

"He was probably only fifty."

"He looked a hundred and fifty. I'm surprised he wasn't put on display."

"We got ticked off by Mrs Lille," Lucy recalled.

"Ah, the joyful Mrs Lille," said Jane, theatrically. "Did we ever see her smile?"

"I don't think so."

"No… mind you, we only knew her seven years – we probably didn't allow enough time."

Lucy immersed herself in the memories. Many friends had come into her sphere back then, but becoming best buddies with her cousin proved to be something else entirely. Never had she spent time with someone who made her laugh so much and who continually got her into minor scrapes with authority.

"I'm not a joker anymore," said Jane, somewhat out of kilter with the mood.

"No, well, everyone moves on."

"I'm a serious businesswoman."

"I know. You've worked hard to get where you are."

"I just sometimes wonder if I've left a bit of me behind somewhere on the journey. Do you know the last time I took a week off work? It must be at least six months."

"I'm the same," said Lucy. "I rarely take time off work."

A silence fell. Lucy accepted that their reasons for an over-commitment to work would be different. She hoped Jane wouldn't point that out.

*

Just before four o'clock, Lucy and Jane approached the loading bay at the rear of a 1950s warehouse on a small industrial estate. The roll-down metal shutters were raised and guarded by a man who resembled a sumo wrestler squeezed into a fashionable slimline suit. He nodded to a middle-aged man in smart business attire entering the premises.

Lucy felt out of place. She wasn't at all sure how to behave.

"Going somewhere, ladies?" the wrestler asked.

"The auction," said Jane.

"Invited guests only."

He seemed confident that they weren't on any list.

"We're friends of Nick Taylor from Camley," said Lucy. "Although we've actually come to meet up with Fast Frankie."

"I said goodbye."

"Jason Hall sent us," Lucy added, feeling a complete twit.

"If you're not on the list, you can't come in. Now go away before I turn ugly."

"You're already there," said Jane, turning on her heels.

"Sorry about that," said Lucy before hurrying after her cousin.

A Mercedes pulled into a parking space to their right. A man wearing far too much gold got out and smiled at them.

"We're friends of Fast Frankie," said Jane.

"Oh?" said the man, raising his sunglasses. "Remind him he owes me two hundred."

"Is he here today?"

"I just told you – he owes me two hundred. So no, he won't be here today."

As they made it back to the street, a smart BMW pulled up opposite.

"He'll know," said Jane.

Lucy tried to look positive, but she was hating every second of this part of their enquiries. If Jane was hating it too, it didn't show.

"Excuse me, I'm looking for Francis Randolph."

The man getting out of the car eyed Jane with disdain.

"Never heard of him."

"Come on, everyone knows Fast Frankie. He probably owes you money."

"Are you friends of Frankie's?"

Jane nodded.

"Yes, good friends."

"Then you'll know he's somewhere in the south of Ireland. Or was it the north of Switzerland?"

"Right. Thanks." Jane turned to Lucy. "He's somewhere in the south or north of Ireland or Switzerland."

Lucy sighed. "They don't trust outsiders."

"No, they don't. Do you think there's a way to gain their confidence?"

"I doubt it."

The man popped a mint into his mouth.

"If you ladies are done...?"

As he headed for the auction, the cousins set off for Jane's car.

"Maybe we're the wrong people for the job," said Lucy.

"You're not giving up already?"

"I don't know. I just feel like we're two little girls playing a game. I mean, seriously, how are we helping

Libby? Don't we have lives to lead?"

Jane sighed. "I know what you mean. It does seem a complete waste of time. What would they do on TV about now?"

"Take an ad break?" Lucy mused.

12

What Am I Bid…?

Following their Brighton escapade, Jane dropped Lucy at Taylor's Antiques with a warning.

"If he offers to show you a bed knob, get out of there. Or maybe get in there. Your choice."

"I'll call you later," said Lucy. "I'll let you know what I decide."

"About Nick?"

"About whether I'm going back to Barnet."

"Oh that. Okay, take care, cousin. Love you."

"Bye," Lucy replied, feeling a 'love you too' response trapped somewhere between her chest and throat as she waved.

She pushed Taylor's door open. Nick was at the far end, sitting at his old desk studying his laptop.

"Hey," he called. "People will talk."

"Sorry to bother you again, Nick. Have you got a minute?"

"Come on over. I'm just looking over some pieces pre-auction."

Lucy joined him at the screen, him seated, her

standing. A rose-patterned vase looked a possible bargain with a guide price of £40.

"What do you think?" he asked.

"I think it's time I bought a book on antiques," she said.

But he was still inviting her opinion on the piece.

She shrugged.

"I suppose if the auction house says it's worth that, then it probably is."

"You won't go a million miles wrong with that kind of thinking. You won't make any money either."

"I've seen the TV shows. You look until you find something worth thousands. Right?"

"Right. And wrong."

"Oh?"

Nick pushed his chair back and stretched his legs.

"Dealers are always on the lookout for a gem that has slipped through the net – the piece of Georgian glass you buy for five, but you know is worth five hundred…"

"Could I ask you something?"

"Hmm… the first time you asked if I was a crook, the second time, if I'd get involved in a wild detective adventure. So…?"

Lucy was a little out of practice at accepting a humorous approach to her questions. She was struggling to find the line.

"Would you mind if we discussed my Aunt Libby?"

"We've discussed little else."

Nick's comment nudged Lucy back into the realization that this was in fact a professional arrangement.

"I can pay you if that helps?"

Nick smiled. "You don't need to pay me. I'd be happy to help."

"Oh… right." Lucy's spirits lifted. "Thank you."

"Take a seat."

Lucy took a seat opposite him.

"My cousin Jane and I went to Brighton to see Fast Frankie."

"And?"

"He wasn't there. Or, if he was, nobody was prepared to introduce us."

"Right."

"You said you know a man. Not on your official list."

Nick pulled out his phone and checked his contacts.

"I'll try…"

There was a moment where Nick waited for his call to get through. That suspended moment of nothing happening – Lucy enjoyed it. Then Nick's face changed.

"Hi, Steve, it's Nick Taylor. Just a quickie… what?………. not without a receipt………. No, I'm looking for a guy called Francis…"

He looked up at Lucy.

"Randolph," she advised.

"Francis Randolph. Also puts it about as Fast Frankie. Might have links to Brighton. Ring any bells?"

Nick nodded and said "uh-huh" several times. Then he thanked his contact and ended the call.

His gaze met Lucy's.

"Steve doesn't know him personally, but he thinks he might know someone who does. He'll call me back."

"Did he say when?"

"No."

Lucy hated that. On the reception desk, when dealing with a complex enquiry, she always made a point of gauging roughly how long it would take to investigate before offering to call the person back in that timeframe. Would this Steve call back in a couple of minutes or a couple of days?

"I'm not sure if I should wait or not," she said.

"Give him five minutes. He's usually pretty quick." Nick turned to his screen and clicked through to the next item. "What do you think?"

As Lucy moved round to take a look, Nick covered the description at the top of the page with his hand.

The item was silver, almost butterfly-shaped, with blue sections decorating the wings.

"I give up. What is it?"

"It's a Liberty & Co belt buckle."

He took his hand away to reveal the details and the price.

"Wow, seven hundred pounds," said Lucy.

"Yep, made in Birmingham in 1910 by Archibald Knox for Liberty & Co. A silver and blue enamel belt buckle."

"I bet that has a story to tell."

"Ah well," said Nick, "Fay and I agree that every antique has a story to tell. We just rarely get to hear it."

"My grandad used to say that when he was alive. He was the same with people. He used to warn against poking your nose in where it wasn't wanted, but if you really wanted to know someone, you never would until you knew their story."

"He sounds like a sensible man."

Lucy thought fondly of Tommy Holt, her father's father. She never had the same relationship with her mother's dad, Albert Howard.

"He passed that love of stories on to me," she said. "The stories behind things. He was a collector of antiques too. Well, he had three items. I've got one of them at home. He left it to me."

"Describe it for me."

"Okay... well, it's a small silver vase about six inches

tall. He got it from a friend in 1930s Spain during the Civil War. The friend died of wounds but had asked Grandad to fulfil a final wish – to take it to the friend's mum. Grandad did so, but she didn't want it. She said it would bring bad luck. So, he kept it and, as far as I know, never experienced any great back luck."

Nick smiled. "You've told me nothing about the vase."

"Oh sorry."

"Don't apologize. It's what I love. Most people just want to know the date and the price. Not that I'm against that. I run a business."

"Well, you seem to have the balance right."

"Thanks. So, tell me about the vase. Does it have hallmarks?"

"Yes – I can show you a photo."

Lucy found it on her phone and showed him.

"Hmmm… do you have the pair?"

"The pair?"

"It's three hundred for a genuine pair, perhaps a hundred for one by itself."

"Is it? No, I just have the one. I do like collecting, though. I intend to buy a few more pieces. And that book on antiques? That's now a definite."

"Yes, well, be thorough when buying silver."

"That can be easier said than done."

"True, although some fakes are easy to spot. If it's silver plated or electroplated, its feel and weight will be off. Then again, like Libby, you can have a piece that is solid silver with hallmarks. The marks don't mean you've got the real thing. Silversmiths used steel implements to mark their products. Forgers in later years used brass. That made what we call soft punches. You have to look close to see the difference but it's there."

Nick's gaze wandered to his laptop. The Liberty belt

buckle was still there.

"How do you value something like that?" she asked.

"Valuing isn't a precise science. Without experience you'll get into a mess."

"I can imagine."

Lucy was concerned that she might have overstayed her welcome, but just as she was about to say so, he clapped his hands together.

"Let me show you something."

"Okay."

"A King Edward the Eighth coronation mug, 1936," he said, rising and striding to a shelf. He picked up a decorative mug and offered it to her.

She joined him to examine it.

"Now think before you suggest a value," he advised.

A value?

"I really wouldn't know…"

"Remember, this particular king abdicated so that he could marry an American divorcee."

Lucy took that information on board.

"In that case, quite valuable. A hundred pounds?"

"Five."

"Five hundred?"

"No, just five."

"That doesn't seem very much. Is it fake?"

"No, it's just that they were produced in vast numbers. Remember, the coronation went ahead. He was crowned king and reigned for almost a year. There's no shortage of these things. In fact, this one was here when I took the premises over. It was being used upstairs as a toothbrush holder."

Lucy smiled and enjoyed the moment.

"What about this one?" he asked, trading the Edward mug for a teacup and saucer bearing the name of Queen

Elizabeth II.

"Um…?"

Nick raced around to the other side of a table and placed the items in question down in front of him.

"What am I bid? A 1953 bone china Queen Elizabeth the Second coronation cup and saucer. Do I hear one pound? One pound, anyone?"

Lucy felt a fool but wanted to break through her wall of reserve so badly.

"No one?" said a pained Nick. "Surely, it's worth a pound. We have Her Majesty's profile, and a most decorative belt of the Order of the Garter. If you look closely, you can read the motto, *'Honi Soit Quit Mal E Pense* – Shame be to him that thinks evil'. How about you madame? A pound?"

Nick was looking across to the door at the back where Fay had appeared.

She nodded.

"One pound to the lady in the doorway," said Nick. "Do I hear two?"

Despite decades of not getting involved in silliness, Lucy raised a hand.

"Two pounds?" said Nick. "Thank you, madame."

"Three," said Fay.

"Four," said Lucy, feeling a twit but enjoying it enormously.

"Five," said Fay.

Suddenly, Lucy felt under pressure. If a mug from 1936 was worth five, the teacup and saucer from 1953 had to be worth… less? And was this a game or would she be expected to get her debit card out?

"Come on now," said Nick. "We're talking excellent used vintage condition with no chips, cracks or wear."

"Six," said Lucy.

"Ten," said Fay.

"Eleven."

"Fifteen."

Lucy shook her head. "I'm not bidding sixteen."

"Sold to Fay for fifteen pounds."

Lucy smiled at Fay. "Congratulations or…?"

Nick showed Lucy the price sticker on the cup.

"Thirty pounds," she mused.

"That's been the price for a month now. Hopefully, Her Majesty will find a new home soon and I'll be in profit."

"So, what have you learned?" asked Fay.

"That I know nothing about antiques?"

"Not so," said Nick. "You stopped bidding at eleven. The first lesson is don't go bust. The next lesson is making money. Maybe we'll get to that some other time."

"I'd like that."

"Big tip," said Fay. "Be careful when placing a value on anything. Do your research first."

"I'll try to remember that."

"If you're really interested in collecting antiques, go to a few auctions," said Nick. "Work out the value of a dozen items. Bid up to half that value."

"And then what?"

"Occasionally, you'll get a piece well below its true value."

"I see."

"It's what we dealers do. It's not magic but we have rent to pay."

Nick's phone rang.

"Excuse me…"

Lucy watched him nod and uh-huh a few times. Then he ended the call.

"That was Steve. He doesn't know where Frankie's got

to, but he's given me the name of an associate. Terry Norton. He runs an antiques place in Chichester."

"Have you got his number?"

"You'll need to see him in person."

Lucy felt her resolve beginning to falter. She knew from her cross-Sussex commuting days that Chichester was six or seven miles away. She was an ordinary person who enjoyed watching TV detective shows. The reality of running around to different locations to talk to various people was tiring.

"Are you sure I can't phone him?"

"Chichester is full of top class, trusted antiques dealers, but this guy isn't one of them. If you phone and ask questions, he could lie to you. And from here, you won't be able to see his face, so you won't know."

Lucy sighed. "Okay, I'll go and see him. Unless you want to come too?"

"Sorry, I'm meeting someone."

"Right, I'll call a taxi then. Thanks for your help, Nick. I really mean that."

13

The Chichester Connection

Lucy was in the back of a taxi, halfway to Chichester. She understood that Nick agreeing to come along would have been unlikely. They were strangers. She still felt a little disappointed though. Jane declining her invitation was far more of a letdown, but her cousin had plans for the evening, beginning with a six o'clock yoga class.

"You live in Chichester?" the cab driver asked.

"No," said Lucy, her mind focusing on whether being businesslike with a dubious dealer would work for or against her.

"From Camley then?" said the driver, referencing where he had picked her up.

Lucy didn't want to talk but felt it would be impolite to ignore him.

"I live in London. I'm visiting family."

There was another way to handle Terry Norton, of course. She could just ask for his assistance.

"Family in Chichester then?"

"No, I have two aunts in Camley."

Nick seemed to know a lot about shifty types. He

obviously moved among them when the need arose. What kind of approach did he use? She chided herself for not asking him about tactics in more detail.

"Nice place, Camley," said the driver. "My mate used to live there before he moved to Hove."

"Hove... yes, I was there earlier today."

"You get about. More family?"

"Um..." She wasn't about to mention passing through Hove *en route* to Brighton to see Fast Frankie. "Yes, more family... in Brighton."

She hated lying.

Perhaps being friendly would be the best way to engage with Terry Norton. Perhaps friendlier than she was being with the cab driver.

"Where do you live?" she asked him.

"Me? Oh, Arundel. I got lucky when I bought my place. Tiny cottage but great views..."

*

The taxi dropped Lucy a short walk from Terry's place. That's how she wanted it – a chance to check out the building where she worked in admin all that time ago. She even walked through the cloister behind the cathedral, past the bench where she used to eat her lunchtime sandwich.

It had been the cathedral that made her go for the theological college job in Hatfield. Her Chichester admin job had been for a private company that delivered specialist services to local authorities, schools, and other public sector organisations. While it had nothing to do with religion, the peace and quiet of the area around the nearby cathedral and the adjoining Bishop's Palace Garden became a much-valued aspect of her time there.

The chance to retain that sense of calm when she moved away from Sussex was a strong factor.

Ten minutes later, at the door to Terry Norton's antiques place, which didn't seem to have a name, she felt a fraud, a fool, a twit.

Even so…

Inside, it wasn't at all like Nick's place. It felt more money-grabbing with large sale cards attached to items shouting '25% off!', '50% off!', 'Rare Opportunity!' and the like. Taylor's Antiques felt more like a gallery where customers could relax as they browsed. As Nick had said, Chichester was full of wonderful antiques dealers – but Terry Norton wasn't one of them.

"Alright, my lovely?" It was a man in his sixties coming through from the back. If this was Terry, he was as chirpy as a springtime robin. "I'm closing in a couple of minutes, but I can stay open for you."

"You have a lot of stock."

"We can soon narrow things down for you. What's your poison?"

"Pardon?"

"What's your interest? Silver, glassware, militaria, landscapes, pottery – you name it, I'll show you something that will blow your socks off."

Nick wanted visitors to buy something, but he had created a stress-free atmosphere that suited people like Lucy. This was a full-on commercial assault. She decided she would *not* feel guilty about leaving Terry's awful setup without making a purchase.

"I'm actually here to see Terry Norton. I'm assuming that's you?"

He stared at her with a look of deep mistrust.

"What's it about?"

"It's about a silver Elizabethan communion set – a

chalice with a paten. My aunt has one and I'm trying to find out more about it."

Terry visibly relaxed, possibly relieved that she wasn't from the tax office or the local trading standards authority.

"Do you have it with you?"

"No, but I can show you a photo."

She did so. He stared at her phone.

"Hmm… looks okay. Are you looking to sell it?"

"No, it's fake. Early twentieth century."

"At least you're honest. Twenty grand just dropped to five hundred, right?"

"Exactly right." Lucy was encouraged that Terry knew his stuff. "It belongs to my Aunt Libby. Her late husband was Eddie Cole. Is that a name you know?"

Terry was beginning to view her with suspicion again. "Should I?"

"Eddie took the chalice from someone in lieu of payment. Are you sure you didn't know him? He was friends with Francis Randolph."

Terry shrugged. "Sorry, I can't help you."

"Most people know Francis Randolph as Fast Frankie."

"Oh?"

"A reliable source says you and Frankie are associates."

"Hardly an associate."

"I'm just trying to find out what happened. One minute my aunt thought she had a valuable antique, the next she was being told it's a fake."

"Who told her."

"Nick Taylor of Taylor's Antiques in Camley."

"I've heard of him. I think you can probably trust him."

Lucy stifled an urge to gasp at his impudence.

"Nick's going to help me once he's finished something he's working on. I said I'd make a few initial enquiries to get the ball rolling. We're not trying to throw anyone in jail. We're just trying to find out who gave Eddie the chalice."

"And you think it might be Fast Frankie?"

"I don't think so, but he knew Eddie and might be able to put us on the right track."

"Yes, well, all I know of Frankie is he's not so fast these days. He's also tight-lipped about the past. Always gives an alibi, even when not necessary. Old habits."

"Not someone you'd lend money to?"

"Absolutely not."

"My Uncle Eddie was an honest businessman and Libby is a lovely lady who doesn't deserve the pain she's been caused. Are you sure you don't know where I can find Frankie?"

Terry seemed to weigh it up. Then he nodded.

"Leave it with me. I'll give Nick Taylor a call if I hear anything."

"Nick?"

"Yes, he's a dealer."

Lucy took a pen and small notebook from her bag.

"I'll give you my number anyway."

"I'd rather deal with Nick."

"Yes, well..."

Lucy jotted her number down, tore out the page and handed it over. Terry examined it for a moment then tucked it into his pocket.

"So, you appreciate fine antiques, do you?"

"Oh... I know what I like, kind of thing."

"Wait there."

Terry vanished behind a display cabinet... and then

reappeared proffering a small pair of earrings.

"I just got these in. Genuine vintage silver and emerald. I'll be honest, I paid thirty-five – they're worth ninety. They're yours for sixty."

Lucy wasn't comfortable. She hadn't come to buy anything.

"I'm not saying you have to pay for information," said Terry, "but this business is built on maintaining relationships. You could call it a question of showing good faith."

Lucy supposed they looked okay. Perhaps the sort of thing Sir George Howard might have bought for his wife.

She tried to channel the spirit of an antiques dealer.

"I'll give you fifty," she said.

"Cheeky but fair. Fifty, it is. Cash or card?"

14
Eddie's Photos

In the taxi back to her hotel in Hallbridge, Lucy wondered by what measure she would declare the silver chalice investigation a success.

What if she found the person who gave Eddie the fake silver cup? What did she propose to do about it? Libby had no paperwork, so the person in question would be perfectly able to declare their innocence based on them owing Eddie a few hundred pounds and offering him the fake cup by way of payment.

On that basis, would it be okay to report to Libby that her husband lied to her? That the cup had been fair recompense for whatever services Eddie had provided? How exactly would that help Libby?

On the other hand, what if the person who gave Eddie the cup had cheated him? What if Eddie had believed it to be the real deal? Would she call in the police? If that were the case, wouldn't any half-decent detective decide that Eddie had deliberately sought to evade paying tax on what he thought was twenty thousand pounds of income? In terms of cherishing Eddie's honesty and integrity, where would that leave Libby?

They turned off the main road onto a smaller road that led down to Hallbridge. Lucy stared at the hedgerow flashing by. Every so often, a gap would reveal something. A field. A barn. A horse.

Eddie, Eddie, Eddie…

A gullible fool or a cheating liar?

This was going nowhere. Her place was back on her sofa in Barnet, back at the reception desk in Hatfield, not here in the Sussex countryside asking silly questions to slippery strangers.

She took out her phone and checked the signal. One bar. Not bad for the countryside.

She made a call.

"Hello, Nick. It's Lucy Holt. Have you got a moment?"

"Er… yes. I'm with a last-minute customer, but it's okay. He's contemplating."

"Right, thanks. I've just seen Terry Norton and he's going to call you if he learns the whereabouts of Francis Randolph."

"Why's he calling me?"

"I don't think he trusts me."

"Okay, but this isn't convenient right now. I'm in the middle of a potential sale."

"We could discuss it when you've finished," said Lucy, trying to work out what time that might be.

"Are you suggesting we go for a drink or something?"

Am I? "It's just that I'd like to get your thoughts."

"It's lovely of you to ask, Lucy, but I'm busy later. Could we put it off until tomorrow?"

"Yes, although…"

"I'll text you if I hear anything from Terry."

"Okay… thanks."

Not for the first time in her life, Lucy ended a call feeling confused and foolish. Hadn't she almost certainly decided it would be best to head home as soon as possible?

Perhaps wrapping things up with Libby would be the best thing. That way, she would be able to get away from Sussex without any fuss first thing in the morning. With that in mind, she asked the driver to switch the destination from Hallbridge to Camley.

*

As the taxi drove away, Lucy opened Libby's front gate. The last of the day's sunlight was somewhere behind the house, leaving the bright paintwork and yellow flowers of the clematis in shadow.

Over a cup of tea, Libby insisted on bringing Lucy up to date with the national and international news plus the weather forecast before committing to their main business.

"So... how are you getting on with you-know-what?"

"Okay, Eddie and the silver chalice," said Lucy, briefly wondering if that made it sound like a Harry Potter adventure. "We've made some contacts, but we have too many questions without answers. Even Jane feels it's becoming a waste of time."

"Oh well. At least you tried."

For some reason, possibly a desire to avoid looking completely useless, Lucy decided on a last roll of the dice. A spot of risk-taking wasn't her usual approach, but these were unusual circumstances. She would treat Eddie as a suspect.

"I don't necessarily agree with Jane," she said.

"How do you mean?"

Here we go...

"Did Eddie leave any private papers or documents?"

Libby eyed Lucy with a suspicion not dissimilar to that of Terry Norton.

"Yes, he left some things. Mainly for tax purposes. He was very honest like that. Even after death he wanted things to be in order."

"Could we take a look?"

Libby looked far from happy but relented.

"I suppose so."

She went off upstairs.

A few minutes later, she returned with a cardboard storage box, although she was dismissive about the contents.

"I can't think this will help much. There's nothing relating to the chalice."

She sat in an armchair and sifted through, although it was clear she had already done this upstairs.

"Invoices... receipts for allowable expenses..."

She flicked through some photos.

"No..."

Eventually she reached the end and placed the box on the floor by her foot.

"Nothing?" enquired Lucy.

"Somebody gave Eddie a chalice worth twenty thousand. Except it wasn't worth a fraction of that. There's nothing in the box relating to it."

"But it must have come from someone Eddie worked with."

"Yes, but the contents of the box can't tell us who. You were on the right track speaking to people who knew him. If that's come to an end..."

"It hasn't come to an *absolute* end. There's still a chance we might hear back from one or two people."

"Who? Are they trustworthy?"

"Well... Francis and Terence are businessmen. They might come through for us. We'll just have to wait and see."

Libby shrugged. "I suppose we shouldn't give up."

"How about some more tea?" Lucy asked. "I'm gasping."

"Yes, of course."

Libby went off to the kitchen. And Lucy stared at the box.

And went across to it.

And knelt beside it.

And put her hand inside to retrieve a tax letter... and then an invoice... and then a stack of a few dozen photos.

She hated looking through other people's things, but it had to be done. In fact, there had been a Poirot episode on TV only the previous week where Agatha Christie's renowned detective faced exactly this dilemma. And he didn't hesitate for more than a few seconds before they cut to the next scene.

The photos were all of Eddie with someone. Each had the details on the back.

Eddie with Detective Chief Inspector Toby Steele, 2010.

Eddie with Billy Brown at his new premises in Chichester, 2005.

Eddie with John Deane at his new pub in Bognor Regis, 2003

Eddie with Simon McCoy, Chairman of a regional transport company, 1999.

Eddie with Steven Coe at his car showroom in Brighton, 2004.

Eddie with Robert Hough, Justice of the Peace, at the

County Show, 2009.

Eddie with Tony O'Neal at the Civic Awards in Brighton, 2012.

Eddie with Lady Theresa Blake in the Winner's Enclosure, Goodwood, 2002.

There were more, so Lucy grabbed her phone to take her own photos of each of them, front and back. She was on the last of them when she heard Libby returning.

"I brought some chocolate fingers," Libby said on entering the room.

Lucy, a picture of innocence back on the sofa, smiled.

Once Libby had put the tray down, she handed Lucy the box of documents.

"There are some photos in there – those he never got around to putting in an album. I couldn't bear to throw them out. I'll get you the album."

Libby retrieved a volume from the bookcase and handed it over.

Inside were a few dozen more photos of Eddie with people dating from the 1970s to the late 90s.

*

That evening, Lucy had dinner alone at the hotel – sea bass, mashed potato, and tender-stem broccoli with a side order of antiques via a handbook she had downloaded onto her phone. It was a lovely meal, only slightly spoiled by two fellow guests at the next table – a middle-aged man and young woman having extra-loud fun. Everything he said made his partner laugh like a delirious puppy. Lucy prayed they didn't have the room above hers.

She wondered. Would this really be her last meal in Sussex for a while? Would she let all this drift into the background? Maybe a few comforting words to Libby would be enough. A brief explanation that Jane was right, and it was all too difficult. That too much time had passed. That it was a lost cause.

Or would she try to track down all the people in the photographs? The Mayor, the local MP, John Deane, Billy Brown, Simon McCoy, Steven Coe, senior cop Toby Steele, Robert Hough – Justice of the Peace, Tony O'Neal, Lady Theresa Blake and others.

She had already located the Mayor, the MP, Robert Hough, Lady Blake, John Deane, Bobby Fellows, Shaun McCray, Eileen Walters…

The Billy Brown photo intrigued her though. It was taken in Chichester and showed a door number above Eddie's head. Had she walked past it during her Sussex admin days?

Over a dessert of chocolate pudding with vanilla ice cream, she googled five more names – without much luck.

Then, over coffee, she googled another three. That would give her something to work with. Two of them had offices in Lewes.

A couple of hours later, she was sitting on the edge of the bed in her room, contemplating the day. It seemed that too much had happened. Being with Nick. Being with Jane. Going to Brighton. Going to Chichester.

Why had she told Libby there was a slim chance? Why wasn't she being honest with herself? Why was she in a hotel in Hallbridge?

She went to the window and stared up at the stars. The majesty of it all. The extremes of universal existence. The staggering sweep of the heavens and the mundane tribulations of humans.

What did she want right now?

What did anybody want right now?

Above, the sound of a bed creaking rhythmically interrupted her thoughts. The couple from dinner had the room above.

Lucy smiled and opened the antiques handbook on her phone. At least she had the answer to that second question.

15
Now What?

It was half-eight on Saturday morning and Lucy was enjoying a fried breakfast and coffee at the hotel. She had slept well, enjoyed a hot shower, and was now wearing a pair of rather stylish emerald earrings.

She felt good.

Midway through her second coffee, her phone rang.

It was Jane.

"What's happening? Are you staying on?"

"For today, at least. I might quit the investigation, but I'd like to talk to Nick."

"So, you two can't stop communicating?"

"I mean I'd like to talk to Nick along with talking to you at some point. Are you free to meet up this morning?"

"No, sorry. How about lunch? We could go over the whole thing again. Maybe we've been looking at it the wrong way."

"Okay, great. Text me where and when."

"Will do."

Lucy ended the call. Going over the whole thing again

was a good idea. By the end of lunch, they would agree that the 'whole thing' had come to nothing.

Her phone rang again.

It was Nick.

"Hi, sleep well?"

"I did, thanks. And how are you?"

"I'm fine. Terry just got back to me. He says he can't get hold of Frankie. Looks like a dead end."

"Okay… but I think I've narrowed it down a bit. Eddie might have had a relevant connection, chalice-wise, to someone called Simon, John, Billy or Lady Theresa… or possibly a Detective Chief Inspector, the mayor, or the local Member of Parliament."

"You mean you've narrowed it down to half the population of Sussex."

"Yes, but how about running those names by Terry?"

"Good idea. I'll leave that to you though."

"Fair enough."

"Let me know what he says."

"Great, thanks. I will."

After breakfast, back in her room, Lucy was on the phone to Terry.

"It's a lot of names," he said of the text sent to him in advance of the call.

"Yes, but do any of them stand out for you?"

"You want to know who might've known Eddie?"

"No, they all knew Eddie in some way. I'm asking if any of them might have given him a fake silver cup."

"Ah right… yes… okay. Yes, I might be able to help you for fifty pounds."

"I've already paid you fifty pounds."

"That was a search fee – and I found Fast Frankie. This is for information."

"Right, so for fifty pounds, you'll give me a name that

might be the one I need?"

"No, Frankie will. My role is purely to set it up for you."

"Right, so how do I give Frankie fifty pounds?"

"Via me. I've got a lovely 1920s wristwatch. It should go for eighty-five. I just happen to have it on offer for fifty."

"I'll take it."

"Just go to my website and enter item code 002445. You can pay by card."

"I'm already holding it."

"Call me back when you're done. And remember, one more transaction and you'll qualify for my Loyalty Club discount. Five percent off all future purchases."

For the first time in her life, Lucy growled down the phone at a man.

She ended the call and went through the motions. She was soon the proud owner of a wristwatch to be collected next time she was in the area.

Annoyed with Terry, but invigorated by the prospect of information, she phoned Libby to arrange coffee at half-ten. She couldn't pass up a chance to ask her about some of the names on her list. If Terry came back with information about any of those names…

Having done that, she switched the TV on to watch an antiques show re-run. She sighed with satisfaction as she was introduced to an 1870 ormolu Rococo clock by Henry Lepaute. That was followed by a 1912 silver half hunter trench watch, a 1910 French Bergere armchair, and a pair of blue and gold Edwardian phoenix ware vases by Thomas Forester – all names she never knew and yet wanted to know. And every one of them came with a story. A great-uncle in the army overseas, a short-lived marriage…

*

A couple of hours later, over coffee at Libby's, they were talking about the old days – specifically, Lucy's deceased husband, James. Apparently, Libby had watched a Channel 4 documentary about the root causes of addiction and had made some notes that might be useful for her niece.

Lucy bore it with the fortitude befitting a Howard, even a watered down one. James had been a gambler and a drinker. A lost cause. If Greg had taught her to fear intimacy through a fear of pregnancy and jail, then James taught her to despise it through his lack of interest spanning months followed by a sudden explosive need for immediate action. It was when Libby asked if James ever took cocaine that Lucy decided enough was enough.

"Getting back to antiques," she said, "did you watch that show on TV this morning?"

"Er…?"

"There was an ormolu Rococo clock, a half hunter watch, a French armchair, some vases… It's not always straightforward telling what's what. A painting I thought might be worth thousands, turned out to be a copy worth fifty pounds. I still liked it though."

"I still like my chalice. I'd just rather it was the real thing."

Lucy's phone rang.

It was Terry.

"Our friend has been in touch. He knows a few names on your list who might be useful leads."

"Which ones?"

"It'll cost you a hundred."

Lucy gasped. "A hundred??"

"Less your Loyalty Club discount."

Lucy smiled at her aunt who looked a little taken aback by the outburst.

"I can't afford to keep giving you money..." But Lucy stopped and headed out of the room.

In the kitchen, she resumed.

"I've already paid you for the information – twice."

"No, that was a search fee and an enablement fee. This is Frankie's information fee."

"I don't believe this."

"Sorry, it's not a free service."

"Fifty. That's my maximum."

"I'll have to consult with Frankie."

"Just give me what I need!"

Libby appeared in the doorway.

"Right," said Terry, "I'm sure fifty's enough."

Lucy reassured Libby that everything was okay while she accessed Terry's website to purchase a rare French pendant necklace for fifty pounds. Despite feeling a little flustered, she remembered to tick the box to get her two-pounds-fifty Loyalty Club discount.

Lucy returned Libby to the lounge and, with the promise of making more coffee, went back to the kitchen to call Terry.

He was quick with the information.

"Frankie says he recalls Brian Rigby, Nobby Reece, Charlie Scott, Billy Brown, and Simon McCoy all being on the scene."

"I'll check them out," she said, making a note. "Thank you."

"Do call again."

"Not flipping likely."

While she made coffee, Lucy googled Simon McCoy

Transport. He was still in business and looked legitimate. Not that she was any expert on criminal profiling.

She tried Brian Rigby, Nobby Reece, and Charlie Scott, googling them without any luck. Lastly, she tried Billy Brown but there were too many search results.

Although...

She checked the photo.

Eddie with Billy Brown at his new premises in Chichester, 2005.

She knew from experience that, for a city, Chichester wasn't such a big place. She had a few ideas of where this might be.

Having made the coffee, she rejoined Libby in the lounge. Then, using the street view function on her phone, she added the door number above Eddie's head to the first street she had in mind.

It didn't match the photo.

She tried another likely location and added the number.

Again, it failed to match up with the photo.

Unperturbed, she kept going.

It took a while, but thirty streets later...

There!

The question now was what would she do? Going back to Chichester might prove useful. If nothing else, she could pick up her wristwatch and necklace from Terry. And maybe threaten him with legal action.

She looked across at Libby, who was lost in a magazine.

Lucy wondered about Billy Brown in a photo with Eddie... and Fast Frankie naming him as being on the scene.

Coincidence?

Probably.

Even so, she decided to try her luck.

"Oh, I meant to say – Nick, the antiques man has a possible lead. It's nothing, I'm sure, but I wonder if the name Billy Brown means anything to you?"

A look of discomfort flashed across Libby's face.

"No, sorry."

Lucy wanted to hug her, but she couldn't.

"Are you sure? I'm thinking you might have heard the name."

Libby was about as good as Lucy at telling lies.

"Possibly. Perhaps it does ring a bell."

Right now, Lucy wasn't enjoying being a detective. Real or imaginary. Certainly, she had never seen Poirot interrogate his auntie.

"If Billy Brown doesn't work out, we could be at the end of the investigation."

"Well, if that's the case, then… that's the case."

"What about other names? Brian Rigby, Nobby Reece, Charlie Scott…"

"What can I say? Eddie dealt with all-comers. He had a whole crowd of contacts, but I never got to know them. He wasn't one of those men who brought people over for dinner. He kept a strict divide between business and family. He was very considerate like that. He was a good man. Good stock. Good standing. The family were pleased when I agreed to marry him."

Lucy puffed out her cheeks.

"Your true love, Libby. They say it never dies."

She considered Greg, James, and Leo… and wondered why she had never experienced a love that never dies.

Then, while Libby opted to pop to the loo, Lucy phoned her local antiques dealer.

"Hi, Nick. I've got four names that might be worth pursuing. But one of them… Billy Brown… I don't know… there's an address in Chichester. No phone number though."

"As I said before, never phone if you want information. It's far better to see the whites of their eyes. You'll spot a lie straight away."

Would I? Even so, Lucy felt her confidence soar.

"It would be great to meet up to discuss all this," she said.

"I'm busy this morning. And I have a lunch date."

"Me too."

"How about this afternoon at my place? Two-thirty?"

"Okay. Great."

Lucy ended the call thinking that lunch with Jane wouldn't necessarily be the end of the 'whole thing' after all. Maybe this Billy Brown character would bring the 'whole thing' back to life.

16

Lunch With Jane… and Nick

Lucy and Jane were seated by the bay window in the Camley Kitchen for a second consecutive lunch, this time enjoying large Greek salads with garlic bread and iced water. The Abba soundtrack had been replaced with Latin jazz.

"Shame it's not prosecco," said Jane, examining her drink. "Oh, I might have said that before."

"I'd like to stay sober," said Lucy. "I'm seeing Nick later about a man called Billy Brown. He might have dealt with Eddie."

"Interesting."

"I'm not holding out much hope. I've spent the last hour checking out a Brian, a Nobby, a Charlie, and a Simon – and they all seem to be above board. I'm sure this Billy is too, but it's worth a try."

They spent the next few minutes going over everything they knew, but without reaching any fresh conclusions.

"Oh well," said Lucy. "If this Billy doesn't work out, we'll be able to look Libby in the eye and say we tried everything. It's just as well – I have to be back at work on Monday."

"Let's not talk of work," Jane suggested.

"Agreed." It was easy to concur that work was a dull subject for a convivial lunch appointment. Although… "Nick's fortunate. It must be nice to be in antiques."

"True," said Jane, "although I'm sure it's occasionally spoilt by an awkward customer. You ever worked in retail?"

"No. Have you?"

"I did quite a bit when I was young."

"I didn't know you were interested in that line of work."

"Lucy, I was trying to set up my first business. Don't you remember?"

"I thought that was selling fake branded clothes from a stall in Brighton."

"Yes, and how do you think I raised the money to set that up? I was seventeen and penniless. It wasn't like my parents would help."

Lucy had forgotten. No, not forgotten, erased. While she was reeling from life's great unfairness, Jane got busy setting up a business. Then, in later life, Lucy passed off Jane's success as luck. She took a moment. Jane had done nothing wrong. Every minute with her now was a chance to repair the damage.

"So, what kind of places did you work in?" she asked.

"Most kinds. I did seven years, mainly evenings and weekends, until I could go full-time with my third business."

"Seven years? I had no idea."

"I wanted to run my own little empire and I was prepared to do anything to get the money. Well, not *anything*…"

"Go on then. Where did you work?"

"Everywhere and anywhere. A toy store, a video store, a hotel, a pub, a do-it-yourself store..."

"A toy store must have been fun."

"It was. I made some great friends there. The customers though – yeah, mainly great, but not always. You'd get cranks."

"Really?"

"One woman sprayed red paint over a display of Paddington Bears, saying it was capitalism gone too far."

"No..."

"Yep."

"That's..." But Lucy's thoughts froze. Nick was coming in with a teenage girl, possibly seventeen, eighteen.

"Small world," he said. "This is my daughter, Rebecca."

Lucy was delighted. "This is Jane, my cousin," she said, getting to her feet to shake hands.

Having exchanged hellos, Nick and Rebecca took their places at a table on the other side of the restaurant.

"I wonder if he's got a four-poster bed?" said Jane.

"I doubt it," said Lucy.

"He's an antiques dealer, so, yes, it would be a spot of Regency action in his four-poster bed. Very Rubenesque."

"He might be married."

"He doesn't look married."

"That's just..." but Lucy's words of mild annoyance turned into a sigh at Jane's gung-ho attitude – an attitude that was all too familiar from their teenage years.

Jane grinned at her.

"Don't look so panicky. In another life, maybe. Hey, admit you're tempted by the Regency thing."

"I occasionally consider potential partners, obviously,

but I don't fantasize about them."

"You consider them?"

"Yes, I'm open to the idea of meeting a suitable partner."

"You make it sound like a job vacancy."

"Could we change the subject?"

"Seeing him with his daughter… it makes me miss having lunch with Ellie."

"I know what you mean. I'm looking forward to doing something with Victoria."

"How about we bask in a little reflected daughter love," said Jane.

"Pardon?"

"Let's ask Nick and Rebecca how their day is going."

Lucy bristled. "I'd rather we didn't."

"Surely, that's letting the entire reception desk fraternity down."

"I'm seeing Nick later."

"If we all sit together, you could see him now."

Lucy was dead against it, but Jane was already making her way across the restaurant. That posed the question of which table would they go for.

She needn't have worried – they were soon heading back her way.

Eventually, with the help of a waiter, they were all seated together at the table by the bay window.

"Cheers!" said Lucy, unsure of what else to say.

They all raised their glasses of water.

"Shame it's not prosecco," said Rebecca.

Rebecca, it transpired, was about to start her final year at school. She was doing History and English Lit with a view to taking one of them at university the following year. She also lived with her dad in the two-bedroom apartment above Taylor's Antiques.

"He loves having me around," she teased.

"It's true," said Nick. "There's just me, Rebecca and the ghost who drinks my beer."

Lucy loved the easy way they interacted.

"Is it too early to know what you'll do after uni?" Lucy asked.

"Yeah… I guess," said Rebecca. "I'll probably help Dad until I decide."

"That sounds fun. As long as you don't get cranks. Jane was telling me about some the customers she got in retail work."

Lucy turned to her cousin.

Jane, caught off-guard, gathered herself in an instant.

"Anyone who's worked in retail long enough will have similar stories. People bringing broken stuff back and trying to get a refund – that kind of thing. Some of them made us staff laugh though. Like the time I worked in a video store when I was eighteen. This guy came in with a fake American accent and claimed to be from the Hollywood Film Federation. He said he needed to take a few videos away to make sure they were genuine and not pirate copies."

Rebecca gasped. "What did you say to him?"

"I said he couldn't be from the Hollywood Film Federation as their representative had been in the day before and taken fifty of our most popular movies with him."

Lucy had always admired Jane's ability to think on her feet.

But Jane wasn't done.

"Cranks… one time, when I was working in a hotel, this guy staggered in claiming to be in Rod Stewart's band. He said they'd just finished playing a charity show and he needed a free room so he wouldn't have to dip into the charity money. I said judging by the booze on his breath, he'd already spent it."

"What did he say?" said a wide-eyed Rebecca.

"Nothing. He just turned around, threw up by the main entrance and fell down the front steps. I didn't suppose Rod Stewart would come and get him, so I asked if he needed an ambulance."

"Did he?"

"No, he just got up and staggered away singing Goodbye Yellow Brick Road, which is, of course, Elton John."

Rebecca shuddered a little. "I've never had to deal with drunks."

James flashed through Lucy's thoughts.

"I've had plenty of experience of drunks," said Nick. "I worked in my parents' pub when I was young."

"Really?" said Lucy.

"I worked in a pub too," said Jane. "At the end of my very first evening, a guy came in and called me a bitch. Then he asked if my name was Stephanie."

"Wow," said Rebecca.

"I expect pubs often bring trouble," said Lucy.

"Drink causes boring trouble," said Nick.

Lucy sympathized. "It can't be easy when people are off their heads."

"It's not always in a pub," said Jane. "I was working in a Do-It-All store and this wreck of a guy opened a can of yellow gloss paint. He started sniffing the fumes while he listened to super-loud trance music on his headphones. I tried to get him to leave, but he spilled the paint all down his front and over me. We looked like victims of the vomit monster."

"I'd have imagined DIY stores to be pretty safe," said Lucy.

"They are, but where there are customers, there is always the danger of meeting an idiot – like the guy who said he hoped my family died because I wouldn't accept his out-of-date discount voucher."

"Wowser," said Rebecca.

"You know I work at a theological college?" Lucy aired.

"Yes," said Nick.

"No?" said Rebecca.

"Well, we don't get any of that."

"So…" said Nick, "have you set up any good refreshment packages lately?"

"I'm assuming you're teasing."

"Not at all. In fact, you never really gave me the full details."

"It's as I explained. We offer time away from regular daily life."

"Where's that?" asked Rebecca.

"At our lovely old college in Hertfordshire."

"It sounds great," said Rebecca.

"Well, it's suited to a spiritual outlook, but how you use the time is entirely up to you. Some people meditate and reflect. Some write or do research. Others join in with the college community, attend lectures or work with a tutor."

"Have you ever been on one?" asked Jane.

"Me?"

"Yes, you."

"I help organize them."

"Yes, but if they're so good, why haven't you been on one yourself?"

Lucy was a little put out. "I don't require refreshment."

"Right…"

Thanks to Nick, the conversation quickly moved on with a lengthy chat about relaxing retreats each of them had enjoyed, and then onto every other topic while they ate.

"I have to dash," said Jane, not long after they'd finished eating. She turned to Lucy. "Can I leave you something for my half?"

"It's my turn," said Lucy. "You paid yesterday." But, before she could ask what had sparked a hurried getaway, Rebecca rose too.

"I've had something come up too, Dad. Sorry."

"Oh…" said Nick. "I see."

They exchanged farewells, with Lucy promising to let Jane know if she would be staying on or not.

"So," said Nick, once Jane and Rebecca had conspiratorially giggled their way out of the restaurant together, "about your Victorian rocking horse."

"Ned… okay. We used to go after the bad guys. Or at least, I pretended we did."

Nick smiled warmly. "Tell me more."

So, she did – about her rides on Ned that led to wild adventures and heart-stopping danger before bedtime.

Nick seemed to love it, although he was a pragmatist too.

"I assume he's made of oak?" he asked.

"Yes, oak, and he has a horsehair mane and tail… and he's painted white. He belongs to my aunt – the one with the chalice."

"I see. They were quite elaborate toys in their day."

"They're more than toys. They're interactive. Only we didn't call it that back then."

"No indeed. The stories they could tell…"

"Nick, you said there were some leading horse-makers."

"Yes… Lines, Collinson, Ayres…"

"And a restored Victorian horse could set me back five thousand?"

"Are you in the market for one?"

"No, I just don't like the idea of Ned being sold to a stranger. To me, he's part of the family."

"That's lovely to hear – although most of the Victorian ones have been passed down through the generations and will have lost all links with the people who first loved them. Do you know anything about Ned's original owner?"

"No."

"Ah well. Good provenance can add a lot to the value. Still, with a little care and attention they're good investments."

"You don't only see them like that, do you? As investments?"

Nick broke into a smile. "Of course not. I love the stories around antiques. I was just assuming your aunt needed the funds. Yes, they're an investment, but it's more important than that. Sometimes, as in your case, they're good companions."

Lucy liked that.

"Is Ned in good shape?" Nick asked.

"Not too bad considering he lives in a garage with a sheet over him."

"Poor old Ned. Having an expert take a look might be a good idea. A little work could add a lot of value. I could give you the name of someone who knows their stuff."

"Thanks. He's been in our family since my mum was a little girl."

"Would she be interested in buying him?"

"No, she died a long time ago."

"Ah. Sorry."

"There's no need to be," said Lucy. "Getting back to Libby's problem though… I know we said we'd meet at half-two, but here we are. Would you be interested in coming to see Billy Brown's place in Chichester? I know he might no longer be there, but it feels like a last chance to get a lead."

17

The Dynamic Duo

Later that afternoon, Nick pulled into a parking space in Chichester. Naturally, they hadn't spoken with Billy Brown over the phone. The whites of his eyes would be seen. Lies would be obvious. Hopefully.

Most of the drive had been Lucy recounting her admin days there. Nick had asked if she still had friends in the city, but this wasn't something she wanted to explore. She didn't like flying visits. Had she planned to come back to Sussex for good, then revisiting her little network might have had a point to it, but that wasn't going to happen.

Getting out of the car, she thought about stopping by Terry Norton's place before they left Chichester. He was only a few streets away. She quite fancied having Nick alongside when she picked up her watch and necklace.

Maybe she would.

But Nick stole the moment.

"Show me your sanctuary. I never spend enough time in Chichester and yet there's so much worth knowing."

Lucy was pleased. – especially when a planned ten-minute diversion turned into a full-blown expedition to the cathedral, inside and out, the old clock tower, the garden, and the secluded enclave of beautiful old dwellings behind the cathedral.

Eventually, they headed for Billy's place in the pedestrian zone two hours later than planned. Lucy couldn't help but glance in windows as they made their way through the Saturday crowds – not to view the goods on display but to see her reflection alongside Nick's.

A short while later, they were outside a charity shop that sold everything from thimbles to repaired furniture in aid of heart care.

"Ready?" said Nick.

"Ready."

Inside, they approached a middle-aged man at the counter. Lucy noticed his name badge: Ross.

"Hello, is Billy around?" Nick asked.

"Billy?"

"Billy Brown," said Lucy. "He's an old friend."

"There's no Billy Brown here."

Lucy frowned. "Maybe he's called Bill then. Or William or Will or Willy?"

"An old friend, you say?"

"Yes."

"Sorry, I don't know him."

Lucy was deflated. It was an all-too-sudden derailment of a seemingly strong lead.

"Our mistake," said Nick. "Have you been trading here long?"

"Seven years or so."

"I'm guessing we've missed Billy by that amount of time then. Do you know what the premises was used for before the charity took over?"

"Not sure. Some kind of business services, maybe. You could try the landlord. I think they've owned the place a long time. They might know something."

Fifteen minutes later, Nick and Lucy were outside Charterhouse, an estate agent and property management outfit on the other side of Chichester. In the window, alongside photos of houses and retail units for sale and rent, a board explained that Charterhouse was a proud member of various landlord associations.

Inside, a young man in a sharp suit was quickly upon them.

"Hi, I'm Rob Greer. How can I help?"

Lucy decided to take the initiative.

"I'm Lucy Holt, this is Nick Taylor. We're trying to locate a man called William Brown. He used to lease one of your Chichester properties. It's a charity shop now, but William might have used it for something else – business services, possibly. He also might have been known to you as Billy or some other variant."

"Unfortunately, we can't give out confidential information. Data protection and all that. Is it urgent?"

"Not as such," said Lucy. "Billy or Willy or William may have had dealings with my uncle, Eddie Cole, many years ago. There are some loose ends we need to tie up."

She gave him the charity shop address and Rob nodded.

"I'll have a look at our records. Do take a seat."

Lucy and Nick did so while Rob disappeared into a back office.

"Do you ever watch those TV detective shows?" Lucy asked.

"Sometimes, yes," said Nick. "Do you feel like you're in one?"

"No, not really. It's a bit strange visiting people and asking them questions though."

"Yes, it is. Columbo's good. He always gets under the

bad guy's skin. I quite like the old re-runs."

"You're an antiques dealer. It's obvious you'd prefer old TV shows."

"Yep, Cagney and Lacey, Starsky and Hutch… and Batman and Robin, the Dynamic Duo."

"We'd be Taylor and Holt," Lucy suggested.

"Yes, or Holt and Taylor. Do you think we'll get a series?"

Lucy broke into a grin. "I hear Netflix is very popular."

"I wonder who'll they'll get to play us?"

"That's a tough one."

Lucy's phone pinged.

"A text from the District Attorney?" asked Nick.

Lucy checked her display.

"No – my home insurance is coming up for renewal."

Rob reappeared.

"According to our records, Mr Brown moved out seven years ago. I tried the phone number we have, but it's disconnected. I do have an address, so if you want to give me anything for him, I'll make sure it's forwarded. Hopefully, he's still at the address we have."

Nick stood up.

"I'm an antiques dealer." He handed Rob a business card. "Some years ago, Billy was involved in a transaction. It transpires the deal wasn't straight and he's owed money. If you could give me the address, my wife and I would like to get on with the rest of our weekend."

A pulse shot up and down Lucy's body.

Wife?

"Sorry," said Rob, "but as I explained, client confidentiality prevents us from giving out any details."

Lucy got up to stand beside her new husband. She was glowing.

"Thanks," said Nick.

Outside, back among the Saturday shoppers, Nick paused.

"About us being husband and wife. It was just to make us look less threatening."

"Oh well," said Lucy, "it was a short marriage, but a happy one."

"I'm wondering if we're in the middle of a crime or not," said Nick. "Have you ever been involved with criminals before?"

Lucy felt this was a good moment for some honesty.

"Only once. I nearly went to prison."

"That's a joke, right?"

Fear welled up and washed away all of Lucy's confidence.

"Yes, it was a joke. It never happened. I'm from an upstanding family, Nick... and I'm sorry for dragging you out here. I thought we were going to chat with someone about a silver chalice."

"It's okay. I do have a business to run though."

"I know. I'm grateful for your time."

They began walking and Lucy calmed a little.

"I'm pleased I came to Sussex," she said. "Even if this doesn't work out, I've learned something about antiques."

"I'm glad. Your earrings, by the way. They're fakes."

"What?" Lucy came to a halt. "How can you tell?"

Nick stopped and turned to face her.

"They're gemstones. Peridot or garnet. Maybe even glass. When the light hits the stone, there's a rainbow reflected in it."

"That's good, isn't it?"

"You wouldn't get a rainbow with a real emerald. For future reference, the darker the green, the greater the value."

"Obviously, I never knew. Otherwise I wouldn't have handed over my debit card to Terry Norton. I hate being conned."

"You weren't conned. You were paying for information, not the earrings."

"I know, but I still presumed the earrings would be okay."

"You presumed too much."

Lucy removed the offending items and thrust them into her pocket. She also abandoned her plan to stop at Terry's to pick up her watch and necklace. She didn't want to look an even bigger fool in front of Nick. She was back to square one without a lead. Yes, it was nice to be in Sussex, but it wasn't her world. It hadn't been in a long time.

18
The H. S. Factor

It was six-fifteen when Nick dropped Lucy at Libby's. She would tell her aunt that the search wasn't really getting anywhere and that it was time to go home. There was just one thing that had prevented her doing so by phone. She wanted to say farewell to Ned. Next time around, she might return to Sussex and find that Libby had sold him.

"Oh well, you tried," said Libby on hearing Lucy's final report.

"I'm sorry I can't be more positive."

"I'll keep the chalice. It's still a nice reminder of Eddie."

"Exactly."

"He was a good man."

"Absolutely."

"He was always doing things for other people. He had a good heart."

Lucy cringed. It was a bad heart that killed him. She knew what her aunt meant though.

"A good man," Lucy concurred. "The cup's a fake, but

so what? It's not a crime."

"That chap at Taylor's Antiques seems trustworthy."

My husband...?

"Yes, he is."

"If I ever do sell it, I'll sell it to him."

"Ask for six hundred. I'm sure he'll go to five-fifty."

She realized she wouldn't see him again. It hurt a little.

"Would you like some tea before you go?"

"No thanks, but would you mind if I said goodbye to Ned?"

"Of course not."

A moment later, she was alone in the garage with her childhood companion.

"What did you get me into, Ned?"

She wondered about paying to have him restored. Libby couldn't afford it, but she could. It seemed silly though if she had no plans to buy him and take him home to Barnet.

Adopting Nick's professional approach to antiques, she gave Ned a good look all over, checking for chips and cracks. In this way, she found a small divot on the inside rear left leg where it joined the rocker. Had she ever noticed that before? On closer inspection, she could see that it wasn't in fact damage. And then she realized that she did know this. Nearly forty years on from her period of ownership, she read the engraved initials.

H. S.

Of course... I'd forgotten.

She hurried back to the lounge to share her finding with Libby.

Her aunt shrugged. "I don't recall it. Is it important?"

"It might be."

She wondered if Nick would know. Could she call him about it?

Yes – I'm his wife.

She decided to google it first. It would be stupid to ask something that could be easily checked.

A few minutes later, having made no breakthrough online, she called him and relayed the details.

"They're not initials I'm familiar with. It's always best to talk to an expert. They'll know more about the trade, the makers and dealers."

"Thanks Nick, I might just do that." There was nothing more to be said, and yet she wanted more. "You never said if you had any antiques when you were young."

"No… no, not really. I mentioned my parents' pub, didn't I? We had an old upright piano that had that jangly sound only the old ones make. I used to polish it and it always came up a treat. That pub used to smell of polish. Well, polish, beer and tobacco."

"Ah memories. And how about now? I expect you have some nice pieces."

"Yes, a few."

She wondered if he slept dressed like Scrooge. It made her smile. Before this trip, she hadn't smiled much – apart from at work on the reception desk.

"Thanks for your help, Nick."

"No problem. I'll ask around about the horse. And about Billy Brown too. I'll let you know if I hear anything."

They said their goodbyes and Lucy tried to make sense of it all. She wanted to spend more time with Nick, but there wasn't a future for them. They lived in different worlds. She ignored the pleased little voice in her head that said leaving was correct because her relationships always ended badly.

Her gaze settled on Libby, sitting there quietly and patiently.

"He said it's best to ask a rocking horse expert."

"Oh, I don't really want to go to any expense."

"No, of course not."

"Well, I don't suppose there's anything left to keep you in Sussex now?"

"No, there isn't."

Libby's truth was absolute. The reasons for being there had come to an end.

She strode up and down the lounge carpet, feeling as if she should be on some mad escapade. It was as if something had begun to awaken in her and was now being forced back into shutdown. She didn't want this to end and yet it was. The reception desk could wait a few more days, and yet it couldn't. She was on an adventure and yet the adventure was already over. It was like being a child again on a summer's evening when killjoy parents call bedtime even though the sun is still shining.

Her phone rang.

It was her daughter.

"Victoria, before you ask – I'm still in Sussex."

"How's it going? Have you sorted out the fake silver thingy yet?"

"Not quite. It's complicated. I was thinking of switching to a horse mystery, but…"

"What are you talking about?"

"There's an old rocking horse. Victorian. He used to be mine. I was thinking of looking into his origins, but I can't."

"This isn't like you at all. Why are you really there?"

"Everything I thought I knew… it's not so clear. Getting to the bottom of it all isn't likely though, so logically I'll head home now."

"I thought your cousin was helping you?"

"Jane? Yes, she is. *Was.*"

"From what I remember, she was always the can-do type. Why don't you call her and go for a glass of wine? Go over what you know. Make a new plan."

"We tried that."

"Well, try again. It's like those TV detective shows, Mum."

"No, it's not."

"Yes, it is. You just need a new angle, a new lead."

"No, I'm completely out of ideas."

"It'll come to you. Just be ready."

"No, I must get back to work. I'll speak to you when I get home."

They said their goodbyes and Lucy ended the call. She could hear Libby in the kitchen, clinking and clanking... and talking – on the phone, obviously.

Ultimately, it didn't matter what motivations were at work. The chalice mystery might never be resolved and seeing Ned's origins through to some sort of conclusion was fanciful.

She stared at the phone in her hand. A moment later, she opened the photo of seven-year-old Lucy on Ned.

Hand on heart, she couldn't claim a job well done. If anything had let that little girl down, it had to be timidity and poor judgment. Lucy's life had been one of holding back and holding off, only to suddenly rush into something and regret it.

Would it always be this way?

She gazed back at her younger self.

"I've let you down too many times. I'm sorry... I truly am."

Libby came in.

"Are you off soon? You're welcome to stay to dinner."

Lucy checked the clock. Getting to the hotel and then back to the station would be a faff. And it would mean arriving in London after dark, which she preferred to avoid.

"Thanks. I'll eat here then go back to the hotel. A good night's sleep and I'll be off first thing."

"Lovely. Eleanor will be pleased."

"Eleanor?"

"She's on her way over to join us."

Lucy tried to picture it. Over dinner, Eleanor would discuss her upcoming duties in the greatest possible detail. Then she would regale them with the shortcomings of everyone she knew.

Lucy decided on a course of action. She would enjoy her meal and then return to her hotel as early as possible. That way, she might avoid committing auntie-cide.

19

Sunday Morning

Just before nine, having had breakfast, Lucy was packing the last of her things into her travel bag. Each little noise filled the room, amplifying her disappointment. She was going home, and it didn't feel right.

She wondered – would going to Taylor's Antiques be a nuisance? Nick opened on Sunday mornings, so she could simply pop in to buy something to take back with her. Okay, so he wasn't looking for a heavy relationship. Would a light one work? She could travel down for... for what?

A glance at her watch told her she still had two hours until check-out time. She could call for a taxi to the station in Camley right away... or take a walk to clear her head.

Outside, the sun was rising in a cloudless blue sky. It would be another glorious September day in Sussex.

She walked around most of Hallbridge, even along a trail that crossed the river and wound all the way back.

She called Jane while she walked, just to say goodbye. Jane wanted to know how things were with Nick, but

Lucy explained that she would be returning home to Barnet and going back to work in Hertfordshire. The Nick situation wasn't a situation at all. She finished by updating her cousin on the Billy Brown dead end.

Re-entering the village from the far side, she arrived at the house where Greg had lived in the upstairs half all those years ago. She paused by the gate. Greg's front room faced west. You could watch the sun go down from the window. She despised it, possibly because it could only offer memories of Greg. Or was that wrong? Was it memories of a lost future? She could see him at the window… young and carefree, smoking a cigarette. The emotions came back. Desire. Passion. Hope. Fear. Regret. Hate.

Thirty years.

Greg's explanation to the police came back to her. Funny how that scene faded from her mind during her marriage to James. He called her his princess. Sometimes though, if she didn't give him money for gambling and booze, he would swear at her.

But he never meant it.

Leo came to mind. He told her she was the queen of his heart and that her breasts were lovelier than any he'd ever set eyes on. One night, when she sat in front of her laptop screen, ready to express her love for him, she found his account had been deactivated. Her brain screamed that night. He had gone because he knew her money was running low. But she knew in her heart it couldn't be so. He needed her more than he needed money, even though it was money to help his parents fight a wicked landlord in Cairo… and for him to kickstart his tour guide business in the Valley of the Kings. She was looking forward to being his first customer. Free of charge, of course. She sat there that night, half her blouse buttons undone, and she cried big fat tears. And she hated herself and her stupid brain and her stupid body. And she hated the internet and the world. And then she went to work the next day to set up a refreshment package for a small group of rural deans who needed a break from the chaos of life.

*

Around half-eleven, Lucy paid off the taxi driver and stood outside Taylor's Antiques. She would buy something and then leave Sussex.

Inside, Nick was with a young male customer. Another customer, a young woman, was browsing. There was no sign of Fay.

Lucy busied herself studying the pieces on display.

The elegant Victorian mahogany writing table was still there, priced at £750. Wasn't that a twenty-five-pound reduction? She ran her hand over the dark wood and inlaid green leather. As before, she could smell the years. How had Nick described it? Bags of character and charm? She thought of letters to lovers scratched by quill onto parchment. What stories this desk could tell.

The young woman's browsing brought her alongside.

"1860 or thereabouts," said Lucy. "You might find one at auction for five hundred, but not in this condition."

Lucy slid open one of the two drawers. It wasn't mahogany or leather she could smell. It was Givenchy. As in perfume.

"I'm here with my husband," said the woman.

"Oh, might he be interested in a writing desk?"

"No, he collects medals."

"Ah."

Lucy smiled and let the woman continue her browsing, while her own attention switched to the Queen Elizabeth the Second coronation cup and saucer way over the back. She could almost hear the echo of Nick's voice. "Do I hear one pound? One pound anyone?" Yes, she had struggled to break through her wall of reserve. But hadn't progress been made?

The couple were suddenly leaving and Nick was smiling at her.

"Hello again."

"Hello." Lucy waited for the door to close on the departing couple before continuing. "You said you had some nice pieces of your own. What kind of pieces?"

"Oh, all kinds. Small objects, big furniture..."

"What kind of bed do you have?"

"Why do you ask?"

"Well... Jane and I were wondering if you had an old four-poster."

"What do you think?"

"I'm thinking probably not. Old beds are usually saggy and having a firm mattress is important."

"Important for what?"

Lucy was losing her way. Why did she have to channel Jane?

"You know what I mean. I just wondered if you had an old bed, that's all."

He laughed. "Well, Queen Victoria once slept in it."

"No way."

"It was after a fancy-dress party. Her real name's Rebecca."

"Your daughter?"

"Yes, she looked so peaceful I didn't want to move her. She was seven at the time."

Lucy smiled. "Does she try to choose suitable partners

for you?"

Nick laughed. "Yes, sometimes. Although I think I've worn her down."

"Same with my daughter. There was a period of a couple of years where she thought she had a role in sorting out my life."

"I know what you mean."

"So... busy morning?"

"No, Sunday never is. I just like to open nine till twelve. You never know. But what about you? Aren't you heading home?"

"Yes, I just thought I might buy a little memento."

"Oh right. Well, if it's going in a travel bag, maybe something unbreakable?"

"Yes... not over fifty pounds though, if that's okay?"

"Okay, I wonder what I can tempt you with...?"

Their eyes met.

She wanted love.

There, she was admitting it. She wanted to walk on secluded beaches with him, and maybe they would have a dog who would run on ahead while they held hands. And not just beaches, but romantic country walks, city walks through parks, by rivers...

She leaned a little closer.

They almost kissed.

But Lucy pulled back. "Oh, I wasn't..."

"It's okay."

Lucy desired him. She wanted intimacy. But she had been there before, and it had ended badly every time.

Change the subject!

"Have you always wanted to be in antiques?"

"No, I originally wanted to run a pub."

"Oh, you mentioned your parents' pub."

"Yes, in Bournemouth. That's where I grew up."

"What made you switch to antiques?"
"My parents went bust and I became homeless."
"Oh."
"I'm over-dramatizing. I was sofa-surfing for a couple of weeks. Then a friend got me a part-time job in Worthing and I was able to get a room. It's a long story but I sold my watch and gold ring and used the money to buy an art deco glass and enamel etched vase. I paid two hundred for it at a market and doubled my money selling it through an auction. Then I started trading."

Lucy decided to be brave.
"We never did have that coffee and cake."
"And now you're going home."
"Yes… I am."
Nick seemed to weigh it up.
"We could have an early lunch. Fancy a picnic?"
"A picnic?"
"We'll grab some supplies and go."
"Oh, but you're open till twelve."
"Says who?"

Nick turned the door sign around and Lucy supposed that was that.

20

A Picnic on a Hill

Nick drove them a few miles through magnificent countryside to a Forestry Commission car park at Eartham Wood.

Getting out of the car, he took in an exaggerated lungful of fresh air.

"This is a great place for a picnic," he announced.

"I couldn't agree more," said Lucy. It really was beautiful.

"If you're up for a walk, though, there's a much better spot."

"Okay."

Nick grabbed the shoulder bag full of lunch and set off. Lucy was quickly alongside him, striding purposefully, and wondering how long she could keep up the pretence of being an accomplished country hiker. This was her second walk of the day and she didn't want him to see an unfit reception manager collapsed in a sweating heap.

"Is it far?" she asked as casually as possible.

"No, we're just following the Stane Street Roman road up to Halnaker Windmill."

"Great," she said, unsure of where that left her.

"You'll love it," said Nick, and he was right.

It was a stunning walk along a trail that ran through a fluttering green tunnel formed by the tree canopy. It was a good few minutes of wonder before they spoke again.

"Do you have plans?" Nick asked.

"Always," said Lucy.

"Plans for the future, I mean."

"Which one? The scary one or the easy one?"

"The scary one."

"No."

The trail eventually reached open fields and, at the top of the hill, a wonderful old windmill.

"It's lovely," puffed Lucy taking in the vista of grassland, wildflowers, birds and butterflies, and views across West Sussex and beyond.

Nick set out their picnic and poured them each a glass of merlot from a half bottle.

"Cheers," he said, clinking his plastic against hers.

"Thanks for bringing me," she said. "It really is beautiful."

"There's been a windmill here for five hundred years or so. Possibly even longer. There's a document dated 1540 that says the mill belonged to the manor of 'Halfnaked'. I'm not quite sure where that comes from."

It jarred with Lucy. Half-naked took her straight back to a laptop and a Zoom connection to Leo.

"Maybe half the manor was covered in trees and half was bare," she suggested.

"That's as good as any explanation," said Nick.

Lucy looked up at the windmill.

"I wonder who built it?" she mused.

"The original was built for the Duke of Richmond as a mill for the Goodwood Estate," said Nick. "This one dates back to the 1740s, although it's been restored a few times."

"It's lovely."

"There's a poem about it."

"Oh?"

"Not a very cheery one."

"Oh."

"It's by Hilaire Belloc and goes on about the collapse of the mill representing the fall in moral standards. I don't know the words as such, but it's about a girl called Sally being gone and the briar growing over the collapsing mill. And then England collapses too because everyone's in desolation."

"Hmmm."

"There's so much history around here. Any windmills in your family?"

"No, but we had a genuine knight."

"Sir Lancelot?"

"Sir George."

"The one with the dragon?"

"I'm serious."

Nick eyed her. "You are. Tell me more."

"Mum's grandfather was Sir George Howard. He was a bit of a leading light in West Sussex either side of the War. It was him who bought my old rocking horse – we think from a wealthy family in the area."

"Do you know who?"

"No."

"Still… having a Sir George in the family. I feel I should bow or something."

"Well, I wasn't going to mention it."

Nick stood up and bowed graciously. "Madame…"

"Sir George set the standards we're all expected to follow. Apart from growing a huge beard, of course."

"Well, I'm impressed," said Nick, sitting down again. "My ancestors hardly registered on the Sussex scene unless you count my gran being a waitress at the golf club."

"But you did well."

"That wasn't family. More some guy called Jack who used to drink in our pub. He was always cheerful, so I asked him what made him happy. He said don't be a lazy dreamer. Back up your vision of a bright, happy future with genuine hard work. He said don't work for other people helping them achieve their dreams – put the work into creating your own life. You'll never regret it. Even if you end up poor."

"So that's what you did?"

"When I sold my first antique, I got such a feeling of connection with the business. I knew I wanted to know more, learn more, trade more. And I knew my wealth would be knowledge. Well, knowledge and a few superb pieces I keep hidden away for my retirement."

"Sensible."

"Assuming I can bring myself to sell them to pay for my retirement. You see, Jack was right. My happiness isn't based on money. I'm too busy doing what I love. A by-product of that is I make money."

Lucy took a sip of wine while Nick had more to say.

"I told my daughter about Jack when she was ten. Rebecca believes in fate, serendipity, fortune, destiny. Call it what you will. She says the right people come along at the right time for all of us. I think she was talking about her arrival as a baby."

Lucy laughed.

"You must be proud of her."

"Yes, she appears in a million photos, but she changes every day. Growing up. We keep the photos though, don't we. Just so we can revisit and feel the love of that moment."

"True, although not everyone keeps photos for that reason. My Aunt Eleanor is researching our family history. She's got photos of our lot with Prime Ministers and what have you. That's where she places her pride."

"Family research can become an addiction," said Nick.

Lucy flinched at the dreaded 'A' word while James screamed through her brain demanding money and calling her foul names.

"Yes… I suppose it can," she said.

"I've got an entire family tree full of workers in agriculture, railways, factories… I'm proud of what they did in hard times."

Lucy nodded. Nick wasn't a Greg, a James or a Leo. She wondered if it might be possible to be really good, long-term friends with him. That way, there would be less damage done if he stopped returning her calls.

Stop thinking like that!

"Nick, you've passed on good genes. Rebecca is lovely."

"Thanks, but half the credit goes to her mum. We just didn't see eye-to-eye on where we wanted to live. Saskia lives in London. The art scene."

"Oh well," said Lucy. "Go on, cheer yourself up with a sandwich."

"Will do, your ladyship."

Lucy laughed. She was enjoying herself.

*

Two hours later, Nick was dropping Lucy and her bag at nearby Arundel station. The train ride home was upon her. She was about to say farewell to Nick and to Sussex.

"Back to work in the morning then," she said cheerfully. "It should be a busy time. We've got lots coming up at the college over the winter."

"Same here," said Nick.

"Well, thanks for the picnic... and everything. It's been fun."

"Yes, it has."

He smiled and got back into his car. She watched him drive off.

She wanted to be with him, in his arms, in his bed. But she hadn't seen a way forward. She almost laughed. At least standards had been maintained.

Ah well, it would be back to the reassuring, ordinary normal world tomorrow.

Thankfully.

She wondered why she was still staring down the station approach road five minutes after his departure.

She might have stood there longer, but her phone rang.

It was Jane.

"I know you don't like to share, but if you want something to happen between you and Nick, you need to open up a little. It's about trust."

"I'm happy as I am."

"Are you sure? You look like someone who would get so much out of a relationship."

"I've had relationships."

"I mean a good relationship. A *great* relationship. Nick might be the one."

"Possibly. Anyway, I'm heading home as we speak. My train's in ten minutes."

"So, what are you doing next Sunday morning?"

"Er... nothing. Why? Did you want to meet up or something?"

"No, I wanted to see how your next Sunday morning would be. It sounds like a solo cup of tea in front of the politics show before a stroll to the supermarket to get lunch."

"Sunday is a day of rest for me. I work all week and I like to recharge my batteries over the weekend. It's not a crime."

"Imagine a different Sunday morning. There's Nick with you. You only get to eat half the toast before he kisses you and lures you back to bed where, for the second time that weekend…"

"Could we change the subject?"

"Sure. Just for Libby, is it worth us making any more enquiries about Billy Brown?"

"We have no idea of his whereabouts and I'll be at work in the morning."

"Yes, but we—"

"For the record, I tried all the online angles, not just Facebook."

She heard her cousin sigh down the line.

"Yeah, he does sound like an opt-out kind of guy."

"Yes, he does."

"Right, so that's it. You're not coming back."

"No."

"Well… it's been fun."

"Yes, it has. But it's time to get back to the real world now."

"Who's to say what's real and fake?"

"I have to go."

"Okay, bye Lucy. Love you."

"Thanks Jane. You've been brilliant."

Lucy ended the call and entered the station. Ten minutes later, she was on the train, sitting comfortably, eyes closed. In her mind's eye there was a lazy bee on the wind… wildflowers… a small bird twittering… a windmill… views far into the distance… and peace.

21

Two Mad Mornings

In the welcome quiet of the college library, Lucy returned a biography of Randall Davidson, Archbishop of Canterbury, 1903 to 1928, to its slot on a shelf.

She paused to take in the moment, which was something they encouraged on refreshment breaks. Get a sense of your 'now-ness' and 'where-ness'. Give thanks for what you have. It was the start of her third day back at work and she had never been more settled. Life was simple once more.

Why chase after hidden truth in Sussex? Anyone in need of a little mystery in their life could find unanswered questions anywhere. Even here at St Katherine's. It didn't mean you were obligated to seek answers. There was that first edition a mystery benefactor recently left on the college doorstep with a garbled note. Nobody pursued it. The assistant director simply added it to the library's collection.

A bishop once asked Lucy if she had ever sought refreshment. She told him she didn't need it. And that's how it felt right now. She had put Libby and the cup behind her, and Ned would go wherever he went. She was only looking forward.

Returning to the quiet reception desk, she glanced at the wall clock. It was a few minutes to one. What would she do this fine Wednesday lunchtime? The weather was exceptionally pleasant, so it would probably be a sandwich on a bench in the grounds. She wouldn't be alone. It was a popular choice among staff.

The phone rang. She glanced at the clock again. It was still a few minutes to one.

"Hello, St Katherine's College. How may I help."

"Can I speak to Lucy Holt?"

"Lucy Holt speaking. Who's this?"

"It's Terry Norton in Chichester. We spoke the other day."

Lucy's heart sank.

"How can I help?"

"Well, it's me who can help you. Assuming you're able to pay a hundred."

Fake earrings came to mind. "I'm not interested."

"It's information. You remember Frankie confirmed some names for you. Well, he's found the whereabouts of one you might want to take a closer look at. Namely, Billy Brown."

"What? No, I…"

"Seventy. I can't say fairer."

Lucy hated him. She hated Sussex too. But…

"Did you try Nick?"

"Yes, but he's not interested in paying for information. He's the one who gave me your work number. Your other number goes straight to voicemail."

"Of course it goes straight to voicemail. I'm at work."

Lucy was annoyed. This wasn't part of her plans for the week or the rest of her life.

"Look, my cousin Jane might be able to help."

"Don't mess me around. Do you want to know where to find Billy or not?"

Lucy usually had a liking for straightforward questions where a simple yes or no answer would be sufficient.

Not now though.

*

The following morning, Lucy stepped off the train onto the platform. A small number of others did likewise. That was the thing with a journey away from London to the college in Hatfield, Hertfordshire. Few were engaged in morning journeys away from the big city. It was the same here in Sussex. Few had journeyed with her from Waterloo to Chichester.

She looked up at the platform clock.

It was 10:30.

She was absolutely fed up with being made to look a fool. She would get to the bottom of this annoying chalice mystery if it killed her. To that end, she had arranged to pick up a hire car from a local firm. She wouldn't pick it up yet though. Her first stop would be Terry, who was a ten-minute walk away.

She seethed all the way there, dragging an unwilling wheelie travel bag behind her.

"Hello, stranger," said Terry as she entered his unexceptional premises.

"Billy's address," she demanded.

"But first, you'll be making a purchase?"

"Don't you already owe me a wristwatch and a pendant necklace?"

"Do I?"

"Yes, you do."

"Ah, now you mention it..."

He rummaged in a drawer behind him and produced a wristwatch and a necklace.

"Billy's address," Lucy insisted.

"You've haven't bought anything yet."

"What?"

"I mean you haven't bought anything *recently*."

"Good grief."

"How about a nice sapphire ring, 1920s, worth a hundred. It's yours for seventy."

Lucy put down a couple of tens and a pair of emerald earrings.

"What's this?" Terry queried.

"Twenty in cash plus a pair of silver and emerald earrings worth fifty."

"Cor... you sure you're not in the game?"

"Billy's address."

Terry huffed but handed her the ring, watch, necklace, and a slip of paper with the details. Lucy checked it and left. She was in such a mood that she was halfway to the hire car place before realizing she had forgotten to ask for her five percent Loyalty Club discount.

*

Lucy pulled the hired Nissan into a space by a hedge. She was opposite the entrance to a lovely little cul-de-sac in the village of Leygate. The first house on the right was detached and would be worth a good price.

A moment later, she rang the bell. She would be tough and to the point. No more crap from anyone.

A downstairs curtain twitched. A moment later, an elderly man answered the door.

"Hello?"

Lucy accepted that he came over as sweet but set it aside on the basis that Christie's Poirot wouldn't consider it relevant.

"Hello, I'm looking for Billy Brown."

"Yes?"

"My name is Lucy Holt and I'm hoping to help my aunt Libby. She's the widow of a man called Eddie Cole, who I think you knew."

"Eddie Cole? Can't say I recall an Eddie Cole."

"This would have been a few years ago. Someone gave him a silver communion chalice as payment for his services."

"A chalice? You mean a cup?"

"Yes. This one has a base, a paten, that you can use as a lid. Did you ever give something like that to Eddie?"

"No."

"Are you sure? It turned out to be a fake."

"I don't understand. Are you saying this Eddie chap has a fake antique?"

"*Had* – he passed away a few years back. He always assumed it was genuine though. Then, last week, my aunt had it valued."

"What's this got to do with me?"

"Are you sure you don't recall Eddie? There's a photo of you and him outside your premises in Chichester."

Lucy held up her phone to show him the photo.

"That was years ago – and I met a lot of people. I left there quite a while back."

"But you *do* recall him."

"Maybe. As in possibly, vaguely."

"Did he work for you?"

"No, never."

"Might he have helped you in some way and you paid him with a silver cup?"

"No, he never worked *for* me or *with* me, so I never paid him – either in cash or with a silver cup. If I recall rightly, he was a bit of a gambler."

Lucy thought of James.

"Mind you," said Billy, "in the old days we all liked a flutter on the horses just up the road from here. Glorious Goodwood... I first went there in the early sixties. Those were the days. I used to pull a few strokes in Brighton too, flogging gear to the tourists. I must have been in my twenties..."

Lucy smiled. Maybe Billy didn't get to talk about the old days much. At the same time, she was wondering how she might continue her investigation. Eleanor had always been a suspicious character. She probably knew far more than she ever let on. Or was this just desperation at having come back to Sussex only to find another dead end?

*

Eleanor was surprised to see Lucy back in Sussex. Surprised and a little put out.

"What is going on, Lucy? You're acting irrationally."

"I've come up with a surprising discovery. Eddie might have been a gambler."

"Well, you would know all about that."

Ouch.

"Eddie was a maverick," Eleanor continued, "but he came from a good family."

Take a chance. You are a temporary fearless investigator.

"I went to see Eddie's friend Billy Brown."

This won't work.

Eleanor said nothing.

"Did you ever hear of a man called Billy Brown

working with Eddie?"

You have zero chance.

"Eleanor? Do you think Libby might know something about Billy?"

Eleanor suddenly became animated. "Please don't trouble Libby with any of this," she said. "The Billy you're referring to was a common crook."

Wow.

"Can you tell me anything more than that?"

"No."

Lucy wondered what to do next. Would she go back and see Billy on the basis that she had established he wasn't a sweet old man but a retired villain?

Her phone rang.

"Sorry Eleanor, can I get this?" She stepped away and answered. "Hello?"

"Nick Taylor gave me the name of Lucy Holt."

"That's me."

"I'm Dominic Hall, furniture restorer. One of my sidelines is old horses. I might have something on H. S. for you."

"Wow, really?"

"This was about twenty years back, so it's a bit vague... but there was a woman enquiring about horses with the maker's initials. I can't be certain, but it might have been H. S."

"Can you describe her?"

"I'd say she was medium build, about sixty."

"So, eighty-ish now."

"If she's still around, yes. I don't recall her name, but her passion struck me."

"Can you remember where she was from?"

"I'm fairly certain it was Arundel."

It was lunchtime in Arundel and Lucy was in a stationer's talking posters with the lady behind the counter.

"It's going to cost."

She sounded like Terry.

"How much?"

"Call it ten pounds."

Now she didn't sound like Terry at all.

"That's great, thanks."

"Or you could have the better-quality plastic coverings for fifteen."

"Hmmm…" She picked up a local guidebook. "How about this as well?"

"Call it twenty for the lot."

"Great," said Lucy. "Let's do it."

Ten minutes later, she was fixing the first of her posters to a nearby lamppost.

> Wooden Rocking Horse
> If you were looking for a rocking horse some years ago bearing the initials H. S. – please pop into the stationer's and leave your details.

She had thought to use her own phone number but was advised it might lead to unpleasant calls from bored troublemakers. For another ten pounds, Lucy was happy to use their message-taking service.

*

Just after three p.m., Lucy pulled up outside Libby's. Having left home at six-thirty that morning, she was exhausted. The cheery yellow flowers on the clematis brightened her mood though – as did the tea and chocolate sponge cake a somewhat surprised Libby provided.

"Are you sure you're not becoming obsessed, Lucy?"

"It's a concentrated burst."

"A concentrated burst of obsession?"

"A concentrated burst of investigation. I absolutely must be back at work on Monday."

"Well, good luck. The whole thing seems impenetrable."

"Eleanor thinks this Billy Brown character was a crook."

"So, what will you do next?"

"I'm not sure."

"What would they do on TV?"

"I really don't think that's relevant."

"It's all we have to guide us, isn't it?"

"We can think outside the box."

"Which box?"

"Libby, I'm determined to help you."

"The whole thing was just a bit of bad luck. I'm not sure digging into the past like this will achieve anything useful."

"Could I use your sofa?"

"You're already sitting on it."

"Just to close my eyes for an hour."

"You're overdoing it, dear."

But Lucy was already leaning heavily to one side, eyes closing, mouth opening. The last she heard was Libby saying, "you don't see that with TV detectives."

Lucy's phone rang.

She opened her eyes.

"You've only had thirty seconds," said Libby.

Lucy answered the call.

"Hi, it's Terry Norton. Fast Frankie has some info – if you're interested."

Lucy suppressed a yawn.

"Where do I find him?"

"You talk to me. I'll pass on the info."

"How do I know he has anything worth saying?"

"I can give you a bit on trust. Billy Brown's success was built on fake antiques and fraudulent valuation reports."

Wow…

"How did he get the reports? Coercion? Matchsticks under the fingernails?"

"No, the old valuer had gambling debts."

Lucy understood gambling debts. James once sold her new laptop to pay off a poker loss.

"I'm not sure where this is getting us?" she said.

"Eddie assumed the chalice was real. He was greedy. Did you know he brought the entire family down?"

"What? How?"

"Invest fifty in Frankie and he'll tell you everything."

22

A Bit of a Shock

The need to travel from Camley to Chichester offered Lucy an opportunity to get Jane back on board. With that in mind, she withdrew some cash from her bank account and phoned her cousin with an update.

Jane was surprised that Lucy was back in Sussex and seemed hesitant.

"Will you come with me?" Lucy asked a second time.

"Okay, but you might not want to see me."

"Why? What's wrong?"

"I had dinner with Nick on Tuesday."

"Oh?"

"We went back to my place for coffee and he stayed over."

Lucy suddenly felt isolated.

"Um… okay…"

There was a short silence before Jane spoke.

"Do you still want me to come with you?"

Another silence ensued before Lucy replied.

"Yes."

Lucy was shattered by the Nick-Jane news but decided

to be stoic. It was no one's fault. She would get to the bottom of Libby's fake chalice mystery and return to London.

Fifteen minutes later, Lucy pulled up outside Jane's place in Littlehampton. Jane was already at the door. A moment later, she was clicking her seatbelt into place.

"I never knew you were coming back. Neither did Nick."

"Honestly, it's fine."

"I might have dinner with him again."

"Oh. Is Nick okay with that? Sorry, that sounds crass."

"Lucy, you and Nick would have been great together. I hope you don't think bad of me."

"No, of course not."

But she did. Very much so.

*

The road to Chichester was quiet, which matched the atmosphere in the car.

"I should have called or texted or something," said Jane.

"You had no reason to."

"I thought it would be another year or two before we saw each other again. Why didn't you say?"

"Nobody's to blame. All I'd like now is that we drop the subject and get back to where we were."

"Right. Agreed."

Half an hour, the cousins entered Terry Norton's emporium.

"Ladies… how lovely to see you." He eyed Jane. "I don't think I've had the pleasure."

"You never will. Now what's this info you have. I don't like being dragged all the way across the county."

Terry appealed to Lucy. "A friend of yours?"

"My cousin Jane. So what can you tell us?"

"Ah yes... Eddie... It was a scheme that boosted social standing while bringing in good money. It was perfect, really. Kind of."

With the end of the Eddie mystery hopefully in sight, Lucy handed over fifty pounds. In return, she received a brooch and a receipt.

Jane looked far from happy.

"If this is a load of balls..."

"Basically, I can tell you it was a financial disaster. Eddie invested badly and lost everyone's money. For another fifty, I can give you the whole thing."

"Just tell us the damned story," Jane demanded.

"Sorry, those are my terms."

Out of nowhere and quite unexpectedly, Lucy felt her inner Incredible Hulk awakening. She picked up a flowery vase and a small brass carriage clock from a display table.

"I'm very tired, Terry. Tell us what we've paid for or find out if these items can defy gravity."

"Okay, calm down, ladies. I was going to tell you everything. I was just seeing if there was a supplementary earning opportunity, that's all."

"There isn't," said Jane, "so get on with it."

"Okay, okay."

Terry tucked the cash under a brass barometer sitting on a dark wood sideboard. Lucy put the items under threat safely back.

"Okay," said Terry. "According to Frankie, back in the day, Eddie was doing everything to rub shoulders with the great and the good. Frankie thought he was sleazy, but his sister-in-law Eleanor encouraged him. She had a real obsession about meeting dignitaries. She sounds a bit deranged, if you ask me."

"Eleanor's my mum," said Jane.

"Ah..."

"But you're not wrong."

"Right, so... one day Eddie was approached by this posh bloke who knew people in the City... Frankie can't recall his name..."

"Don't worry about that," said Jane. "What happened?"

"He invited Eddie to become a Lloyd's Name."

"Oh no," groaned Jane.

"It rings a bell," said Lucy. "I'm guessing it didn't end well."

Terry licked his lips. He was enjoying himself.

"This is where you get your money's worth, ladies. This was a guaranteed, sure-fire way for specially invited posh people, top actors, sports legends and famous celebrities to earn the easiest money you've ever dreamt of. You didn't even have to pay in. You just collected. Brilliant, eh?"

"Remind me of the catch," said Jane.

"Catch? There was no catch. Lloyd's was an insurer on the world stage, and you could be part of it. All you had to do was guarantee any losses made in the highly unlikely and almost impossible event of a record-breaking claim."

"How did Eddie guarantee losses?"

Terry chuckled. "Yes, losses... okay, so, in a worst-case scenario, you could lose everything you owned. But, so what! That kind of mega-disaster hadn't happened since the San Francisco earthquake of 1906. There was no real risk. Well, only the tiniest one imaginable. That's why Eddie and Eleanor put their names on the list."

Lucy was aware that Libby rented her home. Her parents had rented too.

"I have a horrible feeling about this," she said,

guessing that Eddie, Libby and Eleanor wouldn't be the only names on the list.

"And then…?" Jane's raised eyebrow was aimed at Terry.

"That impossible thing that could never happen? It happened. The whole thing went to hell and Lloyd's was on the edge of going under. Luckily, the big boys at Lloyd's didn't need to worry for long. They could just put everything on the Names. And there were thousands of them. It made the front pages because you had Wimbledon tennis champions, world championship boxers, famous actors, all sorts… including idiots from Sussex who saw themselves as important."

It clicked with Lucy. When her brother, Richard, dealt with their father's estate, he discovered he rented his home. It didn't matter that her parents hadn't been homeowners – it was just that she had always assumed they were. It seemed she now knew why. Her late mother, Sylvia, was a Howard. She would have been shoulder-to-shoulder with Eleanor.

"What caused the losses?" she asked, although it hardly seemed to matter at this point. Eddie had almost certainly lost everything for her parents and she hated him.

"The American courts decided to allow substantial payouts for workers affected by asbestos," Terry explained. "The policies were open-ended, so these claims could go back three, four decades, right into the period where thousands of factories never bothered much with Health & Safety. The claims hitting Lloyd's were off the scale. It almost brought the entire institution down. They put their house in order after that, but it left thousands of Names to sell everything they owned to pay off the claims."

Jane hissed.

"What an appalling family. Frankly, I'm ashamed of the whole lot of them. A bunch of duplicitous parasites."

Lucy could only agree. How much of this would be appearing in Aunt Eleanor's book about the Howards, she wondered.

A few moments later, walking back to the car, Jane had a hunch.

"Just wait."

"What for?" asked Lucy.

"We're on rat watch. If that big rat is getting his info from another rat…"

"You think Fast Frankie might show up?"

"There's a piece of cheese under that barometer."

They took up a position that gave a good view of Terry's place and waited.

"Did you know my parents moved home around that time?" said Jane.

"Did you know mine stayed put but sold up to a landlord and became renters?" countered Lucy.

"Do you know what I think?" said Jane. "After this Lloyd's Names thing wiped them out, I reckon my mum, your mum, and Libby all worked hard to give each other the impression they were fine. Big claim? Ha! We shrugged it off!"

"I think that's really sad… and true," said Lucy. "I can't imagine them ever discussing who had the least left after it."

"Rat alert."

"Oh… he's quite a small one," said Lucy, spying a wiry man of around seventy.

They made their way back to Terry's and waited outside.

A few minutes later, the smaller rat re-emerged.

"Frankie," said Jane. "Exactly how fast are you?"

Frankie scuttled away. The two cousins made up the ground easily.

"Not amazingly fast," said Jane.

"You've got my fifty," said Lucy. "How about sharing a little more information."

"Thirty. That's all I get. Terry's commission is twenty. Between you and me, I think he's a crook."

"Tell us about Billy Brown," said Jane.

Frankie hesitated. "Well, I suppose if you two lovelies would like to take me for a drink?"

Lucy was fuming. "I get the distinct impression you know everything we need to know and you're just stringing us along to make money."

"I can't believe you're turning me down for that drink. I've been out with film stars."

"Yes, okay, Bruce Willis," said Jane, "just tell us about Billy Brown."

Frankie weighed it up.

"Billy Brown... well now... let me see. Did you know he got a load of fake silver antiques, had them insured, and then arranged for them to be stolen?"

"A fake theft of fake antiques?" said Jane.

"It's hardly likely," said Lucy.

"It *is*," insisted Frankie. "You just need a dishonest valuer."

"How depressing," said Lucy.

"Not for Billy," said Frankie.

Lucy huffed. "He should have gone to prison."

"He was too clever. He stitched your uncle Eddie up though."

"How?" asked Jane.

"Eddie did some work for him. Billy paid him with a fake cup."

"What kind of work was it?" asked Lucy.

"I don't know. You'd have to ask Billy."

Lucy tried to picture the scene, the actual handover of the cup.

"Did Eddie know it was fake?"

"No. That's Billy's way. Even now, he's got a pile of worthless copies in a cabinet with the real stuff locked away somewhere. Anyway, I can't help you more than that. If I think of anything, I'll be in touch via Terry. You don't want to pay me a little retainer, do you? Another fifty? Keep me at it?"

"No," said Lucy and Jane in unison.

They watched him scuttle away, back into the dark, even though it was daylight.

"Weasel," muttered Jane.

"Do we believe him?" Lucy wondered.

"Possibly. I mean if Billy Brown deals in fake silver antiques… and dear old Libby's chalice is as genuine as the Rolex I was offered in Athens – it was spelt with two L's…"

"We need to go after the bad guy," said Lucy, feeling absolutely certain about it. "If it's Billy, we'll bring him down."

"You're serious, aren't you."

"Yes."

"Do you think we should wear capes?"

"If Eddie worked for Billy, it can't have been above board. The only problem is what to say to Libby and your mum."

"We ought to tell them what we know. Billy effectively stole twenty thousand from Libby by giving Eddie a fake cup."

"Yes, but what about the Names thing?"

"We should tell them we know everything."

Lucy was concerned. "They won't react well."

"You deal with Libby, I'll handle my mum. I already know how she'll react. She'll take two seconds to adjust, then she'll say we might lack money, but we have our reputation, and no one can take that away from us."

Lucy was glad she wasn't telling Eleanor. That said, she wasn't exactly sure how she would raise the subject with Libby.

*

Lucy waited until that evening to pop round to Libby's. Soon after her arrival, she was in the kitchen making coffee while Libby watched a soap on TV. There were still a few hurdles to get over before this could reach a conclusion.

Should she trust Frankie?

Obviously not.

Could she ask Libby about Eddie working for a known crook?

Again, no.

Libby came in.

"Do you feel you've discovered anything worthwhile?" she asked.

Apart from realizing I need to change a few things in my life…?

"I've discovered our family lost everything in the Lloyd's Names scandal," she said.

"Ah."

"I *am* right in thinking my parents got sucked into Eddie's scheme?"

"I thought you were looking into my chalice?"

"Bloody thing. Mum and Dad lost their home."

"Your mother insisted on joining. Eddie didn't have to persuade her. She practically kicked the door down."

Lucy backed off. Libby's imagery rang true.

"I'm sorry. I didn't mean to get annoyed. It's not your fault."

"That's alright, but... um... would it be possible for you to stop investigating now?"

23

Money Talks

Friday morning saw a refreshed and rested Lucy bring the hired Nissan to a halt just up the road from Billy Brown's house. She would be acting alone on this occasion – a last-minute text from Jane mentioned book supplier issues that needed fixing.

Alongside Billy's property, an access road led into a cul-de-sac. From one vantage point, on tiptoe, Lucy could see into his back garden.

He was out there, on the phone.

The way he paced... the expression of confidence. An old man, yes, but a supremely assured one.

She thought of Greg. He had that swagger, that self-belief.

She went to the front door and rang the bell. It was a full minute before he answered.

"Yes?"

"Can I ask you something? Who gave Eddie Cole the cup?"

"No idea. If you find out, let me know."

He was about to close the door on her.

"Are you a dealer in fake antiques? Silver antiques?"

Billy paused, clearly weighing his choices. Obviously, slamming the door in her face was one, but he seemed to be intrigued.

Lucy pressed on. "It would have been tempting to con Eddie knowing he could afford it. Before my aunt became Libby Cole, she was Libby Howard. The family was well known and had money and influence."

She decided to omit the part where they lost their money as greedy Names.

"I know all about the Howards," said Billy.

"I'm Eddie's niece. He worked with you. You paid him in antique silver. *Fake* antique silver. I can show you the photo of you and Eddie again, if you like?"

"No need. I bumped into him a few times. That's it."

"I'm going to find out what happened. I'll never stop."

"Don't. You won't like what you find."

He sounded serious, like it was a threat, but Lucy wasn't about to be intimidated.

"You won't put me off, whether you're playing the bully or that fake nice old man."

"Typical Howard. You make me laugh. If you're so bloody fascinated by fakes, why not start with Sir George?"

He closed the door, leaving Lucy unsure of what he meant.

Back in the car, she thought for a moment. What did she actually know?

Eddie lost everyone's money in the Names scandal.

He most likely tried ways to make up the losses.

He worked with or for Billy Brown.

He was paid with an antique silver cup.

If that cup was meant to be real, then Billy would owe Libby twenty thousand.

If Eddie knew it was fake, why hide it in the loft?

She felt a little closer to wrapping things up. Getting Libby's money from Billy though… not so easy.

She considered the police.

But no, not yet. She needed more information. Priority Number One was to avoid looking like a fool again.

She studied her phone. What to do…?

She called Jane.

A moment later, her cousin's voice was in her ear, apologizing for not being there. Lucy understood and guessed that Jane really didn't have the time for this.

"How did your mum take your news, yesterday?"

"She hardly missed a beat. She said money wasn't everything, and that the family had a respected standing in the community that no one could take away from us. How did you get on with Libby?"

"She asked if we could stop investigating."

"Oh… poor Libby."

"Anyway, I've been investigating."

"Good."

"I've just come from Billy Brown's doorstep."

"And was he a happy little bunny?"

"No, possibly because I called him a fake nice old man."

"You mean he didn't like that?"

"He said if I'm so bloody fascinated by fakes, why not start with Sir George?"

"You think Sir George dealt in fake antiques?"

"I think he was referring to Sir George himself."

"What do you think he meant?"

"I'm not sure. Is it something we can check?"

"Lucy, is it me, or are we in danger of destroying the entire family one by one?"

"We're serving the truth."

"Well... I have an idea. There's a local history group based at the library. I could see if there's anyone who knows about the Howards. Give me an hour to finish off this book supply issue, then I'll see if I can get a contact."

*

Two hours later, Lucy collected Jane. She had received a text from her cousin stating she had a name and address that might prove useful.

"Libraries are terrible places," she said as her backside hit the passenger seat. I had to wait ages before the one member of staff went off and left the reception desk unmanned."

"I see."

"This is the thing with public sector cutbacks that's never considered. Staff shortages mean abuses can take place and private addresses can be discovered."

"So what have we learned?"

"We're going to see Brian Peabody in Arundel. He knows the history of all the big families in the area."

Thirty minutes later, they were ringing Mr Peabody's bell.

He wasn't pleased to see them – even after they explained themselves and their link to Sir George Howard.

"I'm currently writing a book about the British aristocracy between the Wars," he said. "Is that something you'd buy?"

"Er..." said Lucy.

"Yes," said Jane, two seconds too late to sound convincing.

"Thought not. I don't think I can help you."

"Please?" said Lucy, imploringly. She hated to beg but

sometimes it was hard to think of alternatives.

Peabody gave a mild little huff.

"Sir George Howard? Knighted in 1921?" he said. "That should tell you everything. It took them another four years to put it right, you know. To prevent that kind of thing."

"What kind of thing?"

"I'm very busy. Goodbye."

With the door closed on them, they walked back to the car.

"What happened in 1921?" Lucy mused.

Jane didn't answer. She was busy googling.

Back in the car, Lucy wondered what to do next.

"Interesting," said Jane.

"What have you found?"

"Honour... it's origin is in Middle English from the Old French 'onor'. Looks like the Americans spell it right and the Brits have dressed it up with an extra U."

"That's not helpful."

They both began searching.

"Famous Sussex people," said Jane. "There are tons."

Lucy thought. "Peabody said Sir George received his honour in 1921. And something about four years later. I'll try 1925 honours."

A moment later, things became a little clearer.

"Ah..."

"What is it?" asked Jane.

"There are quite a few entries under 'Honours, Prevention of Abuses Act'. It was passed in 1925."

"Abuses? That doesn't sound good."

Lucy read aloud. "It was an Act of Parliament that made the sale of peerages or any other honours illegal."

"The sale...?"

"Yes."

Lucy and Jane were quickly back at Peabody's door. He didn't look happy.

"I thought I explained—"

"Are you saying my great grandfather paid cash to become a Sir?" said Jane.

Peabody looked them over and sighed.

"Yes," he finally uttered. "Ten thousand pounds."

"I'm guessing that was a lot of money a hundred years ago," said Lucy.

"Half a million in today's money," said Peabody.

"Half a million?" Jane gasped.

"I had no idea you could buy a title," said Lucy.

"You can't, thanks to an Act of Parliament in 1925. Prime Minister, David Lloyd George was selling honours to fund his political ambitions right up until he resigned in 1922. He wasn't the first to do it, but he was as bold as brass, openly charging £10,000 for a knighthood, £30,000 for a baronetcy, and £50,000 if you wanted to become a Lord. The law came in three years later, but those esteemed Knights and Lords kept their titles."

For someone who didn't want to talk, Peabody had come to life.

"So, Sir George Howard was a fake," Lucy pondered.

"Not a fake," said Peabody. "A genuine knight of a corrupt realm. Take the whisky millionaire Frank Buchanan. He didn't trust politicians, so in 1922 he wrote a huge cheque to the David Lloyd George political fund and signed it Baron Woolavington. No such baron existed, so the only way the Prime Minister could cash the cheque was to create that title. If you look in the records, Buchanan was awarded the title Baron Woolavington in the County of Sussex for being a generous supporter of many public and charitable objects."

Lucy turned to Jane. "We have more in common with

Fast Frankie than we thought."

"This will hurt Libby and my mum."

"Good grief, your mum's history of the family."

"That'll be the official version. Like when a tinpot dictator writes a memoir."

"Goodbye, ladies," said Peabody. "I quite enjoyed that, but please don't call again."

Jane sighed. "Mum said we have no money, but we have our reputation, and no one can take that away from us."

Lucy felt terrible. "Jane, we've just taken it away from her."

"What shall we do?" Jane wondered as they began walking back to the car.

"I'm not sure," said Lucy. "At this rate, we'll discover our great-great-gran ran a brothel."

"That would explain where George got the money to buy a knighthood."

"I was joking," Lucy explained.

Jane shrugged. "I wasn't."

*

Having dropped Jane home, Lucy pulled up outside Libby's.

Over an early lunchtime sandwich, Libby took in the alarming results of Lucy and Jane's enquiries. She seemed placid enough in the face of the barrage, although Lucy was concerned it might be shock.

"We're not a perfect family after all," Lucy added for no real reason other than the silence was deafening.

"I've never said we were perfect," Libby finally uttered.

"No… it's a shock though."

"More a disappointment, I'd say."

Libby looked wistful. Was that a tear in her eye?

"The family ruined things sometimes," she said.

"Oh?" Lucy was a little shocked herself. Was Libby about to spill a secret? "What happened?"

"It was a long time ago."

"What was a long time ago?"

"It has nothing to do with my chalice, Lucy."

That seemed quite final.

"Okay... so, why is Eleanor writing a family history?"

"She does have lots of old photos."

"The truth though? Please?"

"Ah yes... well... the truth is she fears the internet. She fears all the wrong stuff being discovered by others. She wants to find where the internet information is stored and burn the place down."

Poor old Eleanor.

"The internet, eh?" Lucy said as lightly as possible. "I suppose I ought to get back onto one of those ancestry sites and look everything up."

"You won't find us."

"Why not?"

"Howard isn't the family name."

"Oh? And was Eleanor planning to share this in her book?"

"Of course not."

"Libby, I'd appreciate you telling me everything you know."

"No, this has gone far enough. I really don't think the research you're doing is serving any useful purpose."

Lucy was annoyed. Her aunt was a lovely woman, but this was just plain obstinacy.

"It's my family too. I have a right to know."

"There's really no point."

"Then I'll ask Eleanor. I'll demand she tells me everything."

"No, please don't talk to Eleanor. We need to protect her from all this."

"I don't think Jane sees it like that. In fact, I'm pretty certain she's having exactly this talk with her mum right now."

"I see."

"Libby, if we're not Howards, who are we?"

"Yes, well, I suppose if the cat's out of the bag…"

"The truth, please, Libby."

"Yes, alright, if you insist."

"I do."

"Very well then. Sir George Howard was born George Bonner in Southampton in 1877 to Herbert and Alice Bonner. Herbert's family were rope makers…"

24

Lucy's Next Move...?

After a light lunch, Lucy walked round to Taylor's Antiques on the High Street to update Nick on her findings – on the assumption that he might be interested. She could have phoned him, but as a wise man once said, it's better to see the whites of their eyes. You'll know if they're being honest with you.

Halfway there, her phone rang.

It was Terry.

"I have some more information."

"I'm not made of money."

"It's a special offer. It'll only cost you thirty."

"I'm not driving to Chichester to give you money."

"Use Paypal then."

"I'm really not interested."

"Twenty then. It's good info – direct from Fast Frankie."

"I'm not having someone with the epithet 'Fast' using me as a source of income."

"Call it fifteen. We're starving ourselves to help you."

"This had better be good."

Lucy sat on someone's low front garden wall and made the transaction. She was soon the owner of a decorative Victorian hat pin.

She called Terry back.

"Okay, so the fake antique collection. Billy used it to commit an insurance fraud."

"I know."

"Yes, well, according to Frankie, Billy used the insurance payout to fund crime all over Sussex with a man called Pleasant Peter, who wasn't very pleasant. Interesting, eh?"

"Hmm…"

Lucy ended the call and continued on her way to see Nick. This would be their first meeting since he accidentally fell into Jane's bed. He would probably wish he could turn the clock back. Or maybe he wouldn't. Either way, Lucy wanted to know for herself. If he wanted to get something going longer term with Jane, she wouldn't be any kind of obstacle to that.

Of course, the best thing – at least for her sanity – would be to foster friendship. Lucy and Nick, good buddies. It would be a relief. No hurt for Lucy Holt. Not this time. Relationships were always risky. Her parents failed. She recalled the separate bedrooms… the slamming doors. Then she thought of Greg, James and Leo. They never slammed doors, but they did all close them firmly shut on her.

Entering Taylor's to the tinkle of its bell, she found Fay saying goodbye to a sprightly, smartly attired man of similar vintage.

Lucy stepped aside to let him out.

"Hello, Fay. Is Nick about?" she asked as the door closed behind her.

"He's upstairs in the bathroom. I think he's popping

over the pub to see someone."

The door opened again. It was Mr Sprightly.

"Fay? Could we make that eleven-fifteen?"

"Yes, of course, Ralph. Eleven-fifteen it is."

He nodded and departed again.

"Ralph's a friend of mine," Fay explained. "He's got a dental appointment on Monday at ten. He doesn't like to keep me waiting, but it's only a check-up. He's bound to be there half an hour before me."

"Be where?"

"Our coffee morning at the café. We go once a week on a Monday and do the Wednesday keep fit class together to work off the calories. We also occasionally take a stroll on the Downs."

"That sounds lovely."

"Well, we have to keep in shape. Once a year we go all the way."

"All the way?" Lucy's mind grappled with the idea.

"Yes, we walk the length of the South Downs Way."

"Oh? That..." *kind of all the way* "...sounds a bit more than a stroll."

"A hundred miles," said Fay, proudly.

"Wow."

"It's the Annual South Downs Way Walk. We spend nine days walking one of England's most wonderful trails."

That sounds daunting.

"That sounds brilliant."

"It's every June. We get hundreds from all over the world. We walk one direction, one year and the opposite way the next. Next year it'll be Eastbourne to Winchester."

"Amazing." But Lucy needed to change the subject. "Um... do you know what pub Nick's going to? Not that

I'm stalking him."

"Sorry, not sure."

A silence fell, but Lucy wouldn't allow it to set in.

"He mentioned growing up in a pub," she said.

"It didn't end well," said Fay.

"No… he said he ended up homeless and sleeping on friends' sofas."

"That was his launchpad."

"Pardon?"

"He slept on friends' sofas at night, worked part-time, and spent his spare hours at the library reading about antiques. He decided to go for it and become a successful dealer. Daft, eh? He was only seventeen, bless him, but he thought it was a sink or swim moment."

"Hello, hello…" It was Nick emerging from the door at the back.

"Hello," said Lucy. "I found out a thing or two. I wasn't sure if you'd want to know."

"I do – but I'm seeing someone in two minutes about a country house clearance. Could I get back to you? Um, it could be a while."

"Yes, of course."

Lucy bade them a temporary farewell and set off back to Libby's.

On the way, she accepted that Jane was seeing Nick, and that her cousin was a good person. She also accepted that Jane hadn't had a silver spoon upbringing, with money to help her get started. The truth was that her cousin tried and failed many times from her late teens until well into her thirties. While Lucy bemoaned her lot, Jane worked her socks off. Some of her businesses failed, but each reverse taught her a valuable lesson. In the end there was no failure, only success or learning.

At Libby's, Lucy admired the cheery flowering

clematis. She didn't go inside though. Instead, she got in the car and drove.

It was fifteen minutes before she stopped and checked the sat-nav map.

She wasn't far from Slindon.

Ten minutes later, the car was parked, and she was walking. Having bought a few essential supplies in the village, she was on a trail into the beautiful, peaceful South Downs. She thought briefly of Fay, but no – this wouldn't take nine days.

It was a steep walk up the path leading to Nore Folly. Quite exhausting really. Again, she thought of Fay – this time with even more admiration.

Eventually, she reached the folly – a stone construction that resembled a grand gateway.

She consulted her guidebook to discover that it was built in 1814 and was a purely decorative construction which led nowhere.

She laughed.

I've found my true-life gateway.

The guidebook went on to report that the folly was built for the Countess of Newburgh's picnic parties.

Lucky ol' countess.

The outlook though... *that* was glorious, with views over the countryside, including the distant coastline, Portsmouth's Spinnaker Tower, Chichester Cathedral, Bognor Regis... and, much nearer, Halnaker Windmill.

She imagined a picnic.

Then she thought of Libby and the fact that Billy Brown had robbed her of twenty thousand pounds.

Would she allow herself to give up? Wasn't it a lost cause?

Or was nothing a lost cause while there was hope?

She considered all the information she had. The real

loose end was Mr William Brown. He knew plenty. Obviously, he wouldn't want to see her, but that was too bad. She was coming for him anyway.

25

Hello Again

Just after four that afternoon, Lucy beheld a mint green door set beautifully into a pristine white rendered wall beneath a tiled portico.

She stepped forward and rang the bell.

An elderly woman answered the door.

"Oh hello," said Lucy. "I'm calling about the police matter regarding Billy Brown."

"Oh, Billy lives opposite."

"Ah sorry – wrong house. Please forget I mentioned the police."

Lucy backtracked down the front path, pleased at how this offered an excellent view of Billy's front door – which she approached next. She was quick to ring the bell.

"You again?" he exclaimed on opening the door. "Is it money you're after?"

"Money? No. Well, possibly – for Libby."

Take a chance.

"You were friends with Eddie. You gave him a fake cup as payment for whatever services he provided. Was it meant to be real? If so, shouldn't you be paying Libby twenty thousand?"

"That bloody cup... listen, Eddie stole it and was waiting for me to die before selling it. He had no idea it was fake."

Lucy was stunned. It took a moment to gather her thoughts.

"Why didn't you demand its return?"

"How could I? I had no idea who'd stolen it."

"You just said Eddie stole it."

"Yes, but I only found that out yesterday."

"Yesterday?"

"Yes, when you told me he had a silver cup."

"Me?"

"Until you turned up, I had no idea. It could have been anyone."

Lucy checked that they were being spied on by the elderly woman on her doorstep opposite.

They were.

Lucy raised her voice. "Didn't the police get to the bottom of it?"

"The police?" Billy glanced across at the old lady and back to Lucy. "You'd better come in."

She followed him inside. It was a lovely home, with framed photos of family and friends, past and present, on the walls in the hall, and in the lounge too.

"You're quite safe," she reassured him. "I work at a theological college."

"The police weren't involved, okay. I got into trouble at sixteen and went to juvenile prison. I turned my life around after that, even though I had to bend a few rules to do so. I mean this is life. We can't let a little reverse stop us."

"No..."

Lucy could see so clearly how, at a similar age, she never had Billy's resilience.

"I was just about to make some coffee," he said. "Would you like a cup?"

"That's very kind, thank you."

He left her to peer out of the rear window over a beautifully manicured garden in bloom. Approaching the middle of September, it still felt like summer.

She turned into the room. A cabinet seemed to be home to…

A collection of old silver.

Wow. Fancy.

There was a jug, two goblets, a few different plates, a couple of candelabra…

She heard him coming back and so glanced across a forest of photos on the mantlepiece. A vista of smiling faces of all ages and eras. The photos on the wall to one side had a more outdoor feel. A teenager on a bicycle, a young swimmer, and a handsome young man standing in front of an old racing car, possibly from the 1960s. There was something written on the side of the vehicle. Roc… it disappeared behind the young man standing proudly in front of the car. It had to be young Billy. A long time ago, but, yes, the eyes and cheek bones…

"Lovely car that," said Billy, standing in the doorway with a tray. "Went like a bloody rocket, it did."

"Lovely."

"What did you think of my silver collection?"

"Oh, I never really noticed it."

"What piece stood out for you?"

"The jug?"

"Good choice."

"Good fakes. Unless the jug's authentic?"

"Bloody cheek. They're all authentic. Look around,

you'll see I've got full security, cameras, lights, the works. In my pocket is a panic alarm. If I press it, the police will be all over the house in minutes."

"How reassuring."

Lucy took a seat as Billy set the tray down on the low table. The coffee pot, cups, milk jug, sugar bowl and plate with the digestive biscuits all matched. Lucy had seen enough Antiques Roadshows to know it was Clarice Cliff.

He smiled at her.

"Tell me a bit more about your aunt and how you're hoping to help her."

"The silver chalice... Libby assumed it was genuine, but it's not."

"So you told me."

Billy poured the coffee.

"Yes, so a man called Fast Frankie said it took years to put together..."

"Fast Frankie?"

"Yes, he said you got a pile of fake silver antiques, hired a corrupt valuer to value them, had them insured and then had them stolen. Then with the insurance money, you funded crime all over Sussex."

Billy nodded. "Sounds plausible. Quite clever, in fact."

"That's what I thought."

"There's just one problem – it's wrong. I created a collection of fakes to use as collateral to raise a loan. The man with the money wasn't from my local High Street bank, if you know what I mean. His name was Pleasant Peter."

"That's the name Frankie gave me. He said he wasn't very pleasant."

"He was so called on account of his lovely manner and fresh rose daily in his lapel. If you crossed him, the rose ended up on your shallow grave in the forest."

"Why would you deal with that kind of man?"

Apart from to spread crime across West Sussex.

"I had a criminal record from my younger days. I couldn't go to a High Street bank."

"No... of course not."

"I paid a needy valuer at a good auction house to value the collection and hold it in storage – neutral territory, so to speak. This valuer was given written instructions that if I defaulted on a single monthly repayment, the whole collection would go to Pleasant Peter."

Lucy could only imagine the pressure that had put Billy under – if it were true.

"So," he went on, "I used the money raised on the fake collection to get myself into a legit business. It took a few years, but I paid off the loan and got the fake collection back. Of course, I couldn't tell anyone they were all fakes as Pleasant Peter wouldn't have been too pleasant about becoming a laughing stock."

"No, I expect not."

"So," said Billy, fixing her with his gaze. "Who do you believe? Me or your friend Frankie?"

Lucy sighed. "I don't know."

"Well, I can't really help you any more than that."

"No..."

Lucy took a sip of black coffee. It was good quality.

"Did you follow up on your family?" Billy asked.

"No, of course not. Okay yes. I found out that Sir George paid cash for his title."

"People, eh?"

"I also found out the family lost every penny in the Lloyd's Names scandal. Have you heard of that?"

"Yes. Thankfully, my pennies were invested elsewhere."

"Very wise."

"Let me tell you something. I'm a respectable retired businessman, okay? I worked hard for everything I have – including my genuine antique silver. I never had the privileges of the Howards, but I did okay."

Lucy got up and studied the collection.

"I'm actually getting into antiques myself," she said, admiring the silver jug. It really was stunning.

"Not another Antiques Roadshow nut?" Billy suggested.

"No, more than that. I have a few pieces at home. Well, three to be exact."

"It's the passion that counts."

"I do have passion. I'm looking into the history of an antique rocking horse I had as a child. My mum had it before me, so now I'm keen to learn more."

She showed him the photo.

"Wow."

"You like him."

"Yes, he's perfect."

"We know he's Victorian, but we don't know anything about the maker beyond his initials – H. S."

"Well, that's a start."

"There's a lady I'm looking for who had it before us. I've put posters up around Arundel but…"

"It's a long shot."

"Yes – but I'm passionate about learning more."

"Well, okay, you're not a philistine. I'm not paying Libby twenty grand though. Not for a copy her husband stole from me."

"No… no, I suppose not."

A little while later, driving away from Billy's place in Leygate, Lucy wondered. Did Eddie really steal what he believed to be a genuine antique cup?

It made sense as he hid it in the loft.

She pulled over and phoned Terry.

"I've just seen Billy Brown and I need more information. I can go to ten pounds."

"More? I don't think there's more. Did you get to see his fake collection? Did any of it match Eddie's piece?"

"No, and besides, Billy's collection is real not fake."

"Oh… are you sure?"

"Absolutely."

"Right, well… I'm not sure there's anything more I can do, but I'll ask around."

Lucy ended the call and wondered what next. Was it time to see Jane again?

26

Lucy's Mistakes

In a small Italian restaurant in Littlehampton, not far from Jane's home by the sea, Lucy and her cousin were studying the menu. Lucy had already brought Jane up to date regarding her latest visit to Billy Brown, but there were still so many unanswered questions.

"I don't know what to do," Lucy was saying over a glass of sparkling water. "On the one hand, I feel we should call the police, even though we don't have all the evidence. On the other hand, Eddie was up to something, but I don't want to hurt Libby. If I had a third hand, I'd say I can't see Billy coughing up twenty thousand, whatever happens."

"Not a chance," said Jane prior to sipping her prosecco.

"I used to love Uncle Eddie," said Lucy, "but he was a complete and utter waster."

"Hey, don't talk like that. We're an upstanding family."

"I know. Libby was telling me all about it over lunch. Did you know Sir George Howard was born George Bonner in Southampton in 1877?"

"Okay... so that's a big fat no."

"He changed his name to Howard because of a Bonner family scandal."

"How does Libby know that?"

"She and Eleanor attended a Hampshire and West Sussex charity thing in Southampton back in the 1970s. There was an elderly woman there who seemed to think the deceased Sir George Howard used to be a Bonner. She told them everything she knew."

"Okay... and how did they react to this mind-blowing information?"

"By denying everything and making sure they never went back to Southampton."

"Right," said Jane. "And what about the Bonner family? Do we know anything about them?"

"They were rope makers."

"Rope makers? I wonder why my mother never mentioned it."

Lucy checked her phone's notepad where she had typed a few details.

"George's parents were Herbert and Alice Bonner. Herbert turned his trade into a successful business and became a wealthy merchant. He even encouraged his daughter Isobel, George's sister, to seduce a lord."

"What? Even though she was from a ropey family?"

"Alas, this lord was committed to an arranged marriage."

"He was already tied up?"

"Yes, with an upper-class woman. George obviously saw his sister's pain and vowed to do something drastic."

"You mean join the upper classes himself?"

"Yes, but around 1900, his equally upwardly-mobile dad became embroiled in a political bribery case – so, George left Southampton and changed his surname."

Jane nodded. "And then spent the next couple of decades establishing himself in Camley, growing a beard, and dreaming of becoming a knight."

They both took a sip of their drinks.

"I hate him," said Jane.

"Me too," said Lucy, "but I think I understand him a little better."

"Understanding people is a good start."

"Yes, it is."

They stared at each other. Two cousins. Two strangers in many ways, but in so many fewer ways than a week ago.

"I'm sorry for any bad feeling over the years," said Lucy. "It's my fault. I think I struggled with being a grown-up."

"I'll accept your apology if you accept mine. I was so busy hurtling forward, I never bothered to look behind to see if anyone had fallen overboard. I was completely self-absorbed."

Lucy raised her glass.

"Let's put the past in its place."

Jane clinked it.

"To a friendship that is roaring all the way back to its best."

They drank to each other then put their glasses down.

"I remember when you got into trouble," said Jane. "My parents said keep away from Lucy. She'll drag you into trouble too."

"Hey, back when we were teens, you had a dozen boyfriends. Me and Greg only did it once and I thought I was going to die of embarrassment. He said I was hopeless. And then…" But the life drained from Lucy's voice as the memories crowded in. "And then… nights I couldn't sleep… just this one blinding thought of being pregnant in prison... and wondering how much longer I could take it."

"That's terrible. I wish I'd known."

"Nobody knew."

"Lucy... don't think bad of me, but I hardly gave it a second thought."

"I give it endless thoughts sometimes. I helped him move a load of booze from his place to a nearby garage. He said a friend brought it over from France – a booze cruise. Everyone was doing it back then, bringing a few cases of wine back to save on the tax. I later learned it was half a million pounds worth of stolen Scotch, gin and vodka from a depot in London. The thing is... I wanted to be a police officer."

"Oh, I never knew."

"I never said."

"Right... but you were seventeen. There was nothing to stop you when you were twenty-five, say."

"No, I ran empty on integrity that day. For years, I worried other people could see it in me, that lack of the right stuff."

"So, you told yourself you wouldn't join the police force. It was just a decision. It wasn't the end of the world."

"I didn't tell me I wouldn't join the police."

"Who did?"

"I was seventeen. Bloody stupid and naive. I'd never spent the night with a man before. I thought I was being so grown up. Deep down, I guessed Greg was dealing in stolen goods, but I persuaded myself he was a victim of circumstances. I worked out that my influence would bring him back to the right side of the law. It all fitted in with my life up to that exact moment. You see, I was becoming a fully mature woman, I had an exciting boyfriend I would transform where you'd failed, I was going to join the police force, and... the doorbell rang."

"The doorbell...?"

"It was the police. I didn't realize they were arresting Greg for dealing Class A drugs as well as the booze. I was in the bedroom upstairs semi-naked wondering what was going on. Then a police officer came in and arrested me. I understood his words, but nothing made sense. When they put me in the back of a police car with Greg, he seemed to find it funny. He even told the two officers in the front that I was going to join the force. One of them said the police didn't take drug-dealing trash. I almost threw up with panic. When we got to the police station, they had four others from Greg's gang. I was in meltdown. I just cried for my mum and dad. And then I realized I couldn't call them. The thought of my mum having to come to the police station... she was on a charity committee with the deputy chief constable. It would've been a betrayal."

"So, you never called anyone?"

"I lied that I was eighteen and so didn't need a parent there. It all came out a few weeks later when Mum opened a letter to me from my solicitor."

"That's awful, Lucy. I'm sorry you went through all that by yourself. I mean, Greg... he was fun for a time... but then I began to see how seriously bad he was. I remember asking you to stay away."

"The police wanted to know how I got to know him. I couldn't tell them you introduced us, so I lied."

"I know, but neither of us needed to be involved with him."

Over the years, Lucy had recalled the events many times. It always came across as one girl showing off her boyfriend, and then becoming annoyed when he switched allegiance. Now it came over for exactly what it was. One friend trying to help another stay out of trouble.

"My evidence helped put him in jail, while I got off," Lucy said quietly.

"You and six others gave evidence. And the police found ten grand's worth of cocaine under that bed you were arrested on. Don't beat yourself up. You were young."

"Young? I went wrong again with James."

Jane nodded sympathetically. "I know."

"And then there was a man called Leo."

"I know – he fleeced you for seven grand."

Lucy was stunned. "How… how do you know?"

"Your Victoria tweeted my Ellie in the strictest confidence, and Ellie started telling me in the strictest confidence as she was coming in one day… except my mum was in the kitchen. So, basically, everyone knows."

Ice cold dread seeped into Lucy's veins.

"Everyone?"

"Yes, everyone knows you're a convicted gangster's bit of fluff, an alcoholic gambler's excuse-maker, and a semi-naked scam victim… everyone thinks you're an idiot. For the record, I don't."

Lucy couldn't get out of the restaurant fast enough. Somewhere in the background, her cousin's voice… but she was jogging now.

Back in the car, she roared out of Littlehampton bound for the hotel, where she would grab her things and get back to Chichester to hand in the hire car.

She switched the radio on. Classical music. Violin and piano. Mozart, she guessed. A glance at the infotainment screen told her it was Beethoven.

Can't even get that right.

She recalled a silly thing. Nick calling her his wife.

Why did that hurt now? He wasn't serious at the time and seemed happy enough living solo. Had she unwittingly disturbed that acceptance of a single life and then not been there when he was ready to respond?

It didn't matter. Any reason to be in Sussex now was dead.

She wiped her eyes to clear her vision.

Her phone rang.

Jane? Nick?

She pulled over to answer.

As it was, she didn't recognize the number. She wouldn't be changing her plans for Nick or for Jane, or for Libby, Eleanor, Terry or Frankie.

She answered anyway.

"Hello?"

"Hello, is that Lucy?"

It was an elderly woman's voice.

"Yes, it's Lucy. Who's speaking?"

"I'm Virginia Kirby. I saw your poster on a lamppost. A poster about a horse."

Lucy's brain was fried. "A horse?"

"Yes, with the initials H. S."

"I'm about to pack it all in. But... um... where are you?"

"I'm in Arundel."

Lucy felt that the whole world was laughing at her, but she had no choice. Ned was only an old rocking horse but letting him down now would surely be the absolute final nail in her self-worth.

27

Virginia

It was a sunny Saturday morning that offered motorists the finest views of Sussex – except that, while driving, Lucy's thoughts were on the previous evening where a few drinks by herself at the hotel bar had led to her calling Nick. He was polite, saying that he still had a date lined up with Jane. He was sorry things got messed up. He wished it hadn't been so. He had shut down his heart. Lucy opened it. He did need someone in his life.

Well, no, he hadn't said any of that. She dreamed it up while waiting for his voicemail to do its thing. She ended up leaving a message along the lines of, "Hi, it's Lucy. I'll call tomorrow."

She parked the car outside a row of small cottages in Arundel. These were early buildings, possibly pre-Victorian, and at odds with the modern structure next door. She stepped up to a cherry gloss door in the middle of the row and rang the bell. A small dog commenced yapping in earnest. Lucy guessed Yorkshire Terrier or possibly Jack Russell.

The door opened and Lucy was greeted by an elderly

lady in a thick red cardigan... and a Yorkshire Terrier.

"I'm Virginia. You must be Lucy."

"That's right. Would you like me to show you some ID?"

"Don't be silly. Come in, come in."

Lucy tutted to herself and followed the old lady into her tiny lounge. The yapping dog followed them all the way but quietened once it had jumped up onto the sofa.

"Thanks for getting in touch," said Lucy. "I'd all but forgotten about the posters."

"It certainly surprised me to see someone asking about the horse. Now, how about some tea?"

It took five minutes to sort out the pot of Earl Grey, the chocolate digestive biscuits, the slice of lemon drizzle cake and the business of bringing it all into the lounge on a tray. Twice Lucy offered to help – or take over – but she was rebuffed both times.

Eventually, the two of them were facing each other over a small table armed with bone china cups. Lucy sipped her tea and then attempted to launch her series of questions.

"Do have a biscuit," said Virginia, frustrating her. "And the cake is delicious. Don't miss out."

Lucy took a biscuit.

"Thank you. Um... could I ask you about the rocking horse?"

"That's why you're here. Why don't you tell me your story first, and then I'll tell you mine?"

"Okay," said Lucy. "I had the horse when I was a little girl in the late seventies, early eighties. My mum had him in the early fifties. What would be wonderful would be to learn more about Ned's life before we got him."

"Ned?"

"It's the name we gave him."

"Ah… Ned. Good name. Solid, dependable Ned. Yes, I can see that. Are you sure you won't have a piece of cake?"

"No, really. So, before the 1950s…?"

Virginia seemed to rummage through the available information in her head. Lucy was praying that this lovely old lady would be able to take Ned's story all the way back to his Victorian creation, although that seemed unlikely.

"Yes, so… before the 1950s… I can take you back to the War when I was a girl."

Lucy did a quick calculation. Virginia had to be in her early eighties.

"Was he a gift?" she asked.

"Yes, very much so. I don't suppose you have a photo?"

"Oh… yes, of course."

Lucy pulled her phone out and called up the shot of her on Ned all those years ago.

"Ohh," Virginia gasped. "My dear, dear Rocinante."

Lucy tried to understand what Virginia had said.

Ross… ee… naan… tay?

"Sorry, what did you say?" she asked.

"The horse," said Virginia. "He's called Rocinante. At least, he was in the 1940s."

Lucy was delighted. They were getting somewhere.

"I'm jealous," said Virginia. "We never had a camera back then."

"What a pity," said Lucy. "That would have been something special."

"Yes… difficult days…"

Virginia fell silent.

Lucy left it a moment before prompting her.

"Can you tell me more?"

"Rocinante was mine for a while, then he went to my cousin, and then came back to my younger brother. We were separated for good in 1950 when we couldn't afford a rent increase and fell on hard times."

"Oh, that's a sad thing to hear."

"It hurt but we had to move out of our lovely cottage in Camley into a single room and sell what little we had to stay afloat."

Virginia fell silent again.

"Um, his name?" Lucy asked. "Rocinante?"

Virginia sprang up and headed for a small bookcase. She retrieved an old volume and handed it to Lucy before retaking her seat.

"When I say we sold everything to stay afloat, I kept hold of that."

The book was *Don Quixote* by Miguel de Cervantes.

Don Key-ho-tay. She knew the song by Nick Kershaw. She used to sing along with it on the radio when she was… eleven… twelve…? Here was the book though. The real thing. Lucy put it down on the coffee table.

"The book must be very special to you."

"It is. For me, Rocinante is literature's finest horse. He's not exceptional, but he reflects Don Quixote, his master. They're both a little past their prime. He's not a shining steed. Rocinante does what he can to earn the greatness that befits a beast doing the bidding of Don Quixote, but they're both engaged in a task beyond their capabilities."

"Ah well," said Lucy, "We're all prone to getting dragged into that."

"My grandfather was a fan of Don Quixote. He used to tell me the stories as I rode Rocinante. He wasn't really a great horse, but he wanted to be. He strove to be. He was like most of us. *Rocín* means 'workhorse'. *Ante* means 'before' or 'previously'. So *Rocinante* means previously being a *rocín*, before becoming a steed grand enough to carry the great Don Quixote."

"Do you know who bought him from you?"

"Yes, our landlord. He took him because my mum owed a lot in rent."

Lucy had a bad feeling.

"Who was your landlord?"

"Oh, he was quite a figure in the community. Sir George Howard."

Lucy's heart sank.

Her beloved Ned, supposedly bought from a wealthy family whose children had grown up... in reality, torn from a poor family at their most vulnerable.

Heartless.

"Virginia, what do you know of Rocinante's origins? Do you know anything about when he was made?"

"Yes, he was made by my grandfather in 1943."

"Your...? But... Ned's Victorian." Another Howard lie struck down. "He's not Victorian..."

"He was built during the War. You must understand that I was very young at the time, but I can tell you those were difficult years for the family with my father in the army. My grandad was a carpenter, an amateur artist, and a volunteer air raid warden. His patrol area included a small museum. The museum was actually closed for the War, but he got friendly with the man looking after the building. When the Nazis weren't dropping bombs, Grandad would get access to the exhibits as he loved to draw them. The one he loved most was a Victorian rocking horse from the 1860s. Another biscuit?"

"Oh... yes, thank you. Please, carry on."

"Yes, so... Grandad decided to build a copy of this horse in every detail. It took him over a year to get it right

— as I said, he had other duties. It wasn't easy either. Early on, a German bomb destroyed the museum, so he had to work from his drawings. And then, halfway through, another bomb destroyed a cinema. Grandad's sister was among a hundred people killed."

Lucy shared a moment of silence before Virginia continued.

"Rocinante was originally called Edith, after Grandad's sister, but that only lasted a week. He decided he wanted children to have fun on the horse, not be drawn back to tragedy. So, Edith became Rocinante."

"What was your grandad's name?"

Henry Stafford.

H. S.

Lucy gave up. Some antiques simply shouldn't be separated from the people who made and loved them.

Her phone pinged. It was a text from Fast Frankie.

She ignored it.

"You were looking for Ned twenty years ago."

"Yes, I knew where he went seventy years ago but I lost touch. My hope twenty years ago was that he might have come onto the market. My grandson's seventh birthday, you see... He's twenty-seven now and lives on the twentieth floor of an apartment block near Canary Wharf."

"Ah, not likely to be interested in a rocking horse then."

"No."

"Was that the last you had to do with Sir George?"

"Not at all. When I was fourteen, I began working for him as a servant. Well, we were still living in a single room. He was still our landlord, you see. My brother worked for him too some years later as a gardener. My cousin too. He could fix anything."

"I see."

"I remember one of my first tasks... I was sent to Sir George's son's house to serve food and drinks at a lunch party. There was a little girl called Sylvia riding Rocinante. She told me he had a new name. I cried my eyes out. Not just for the horse, but the life I once knew."

Lucy felt a part of her soul shrinking. With each passing second, she despised her family more and more.

Virginia continued, "I went to see Sir George's son..."

"Albert," Lucy added.

"Yes, that's right – Albert. I offered to work extra hours to buy the horse back. He refused. He said Ned... yes, it was Ned. Thank you for reminding me, Lucy. He said Ned was his daughter's prized possession. Sylvia would have been six or seven, so I couldn't blame her."

Lucy felt ashamed. She never knew any of this. Albert, her grandfather, told her the horse had been in the family for generations.

She gazed on Virginia.

We were the great family. You were the servants.

"Lucy, did you love our horse as much as I did?" Virginia asked.

"I'm not so sure now, but yes. Ned and I... we had an arrangement. We used to go after the bad guys."

"Oh, how lovely," said Virginia, clapping her hands together. "Do tell me more."

Lucy recounted how her grandad – on her father's side! – loved stories about the Wild West, and how they seeped into young Lucy's adventures with Ned. In turn, Lucy asked Virginia if adventures had been her thing.

"Yes, we went on adventures too – through valleys, across rivers, into the mountains... I think though, I came to understand something more important. There's a line in Don Quixote that goes something like, 'as Rocinante went down, our gallant hero went over his head, and after he had struck the ground he rolled for some distance.' Years later, I came to see that riding Rocinante was just like life – it could throw you, but you had to get back on the horse. And life did throw me, especially when my father never survived the Normandy landings."

Lucy felt a lurch in her stomach.

"I can see the horse meant a lot to you."

"To me, my brother and our cousin."

"Virginia… I'd like to give Ned… Rocinante back to you."

"You own him?"

No, but I should be able to buy him.

"He lives with my aunt."

"Let me pour you some more tea."

While Virginia did so, Lucy checked the text from Frankie.

'Let's get even with Billy.'

Lucy wondered. Would getting even with Billy be right or wrong?

Or perhaps both?

28

Frankie's Way

Ten minutes before Lucy was due to meet Frankie, she was sitting on a bench in the covered cloister walkway behind Chichester Cathedral.

The years fell away as chewed slowly on a cheese salad baguette while reading about Don Quixote on her phone. Her admin role just up the road had been a decent enough job, but the time she got to sit here or in the adjoining garden had always filled her with a feeling of peace and calm.

And calm was exactly what she needed. She had yet to call Jane or Victoria. There was a distinct need to talk to both of them, but it seemed so much easier to put it off.

She closed her eyes. She wasn't one for meditation, but this was close. An age seemed to pass. Maybe she would never be disturbed from this all-encompassing, calming peace…

"Oi."

Lucy opened her eyes. It was Frankie, standing over her, leering.

She checked her watch. He was bang on time.

"I have to see someone first," he said. "It won't take long."

She nodded and rose from the bench to follow him, only stopping for a second at the waste bin to discard her half-eaten baguette.

Her opinion of Fast Frankie had not been high since first hearing of him. The more she got to know him, however, the more she came to understand that he wasn't someone you either liked or didn't. He was a facilitator – the gooey oil that kept the machinery of the semi-criminal world running. It wasn't a matter of having an opinion of him. All you needed was a simple grasp of two factors:

1) was his information value for money?

2) would his advice land you in jail?

"By the way," she said. "Billy told me your version of events is all lies."

"Don't tell me," Frankie scoffed, "Billy was charming and lovely. Why don't you have 'gullible' stamped on your forehead? The man's a crook."

"I'm having trouble telling who's a crook and who isn't."

"I'm the only one you can trust. We'll get justice by the back door, okay? That low-life owes Libby twenty grand, remember."

To Lucy, listening to Frankie was like entering a darkened room. You couldn't be certain of what you were letting yourself in for. He had a point though. The likelihood was that Eddie – for whatever reason – brought home what he thought was a genuine antique. Did he steal it? Lucy couldn't be sure. But if he had earned it... what services did he provide for a man like Billy Brown?

At the end of it all though... in the absolute final analysis... she found it hard to overlook the fact that Billy was living a very nice life, whereas Libby had been denied a move to Selsey. It didn't seem fair.

A few minutes later, they were out of the cathedral's calming quarter and among the ambling ranks of Saturday shoppers. Lucy glanced at her reflection as they passed a baker's. Seven days ago, Chichester's glass reflected a possible future: herself and Nick together. Now it showed her associating with a man who was almost certainly a villain.

"This is an important meet," said Frankie, as she followed him into an alley. "Top people."

She sensed he was showing off. He was too insubstantial to know any top people. He seemed to believe in himself though and even took on a swagger as he pulled out his phone and made a call.

Up ahead, a door on the right near the end of the alley was guarded by two huge bald men in shiny suits. They reminded Lucy of the gorilla she and Jane had encountered in Brighton back at the start of the investigation.

"Yo, Big Arnie, how's it going?" Frankie said into his phone. "Sweet... seventy grand for a Merc... like it."

Lucy had the distinct impression his call was to the Speaking Clock.

"Yeah, I'll try him," Frankie continued, "see if he knows anyone."

They reached the doormen, who looked quite vicious up close.

Frankie tried to walk past but found his way blocked by a meaty hand.

"Yeah, hang on," he said into the phone, "I'm being held up by a couple of bald mugs."

Oh crap, we're not getting out alive.

One of the doormen took Frankie's phone off him,

listened, and reported back to him.

"Big Arnie says the time sponsored by 4U Media is 12:38 and ten seconds." He returned the phone. "The street is back the way you came. Have a nice day."

Lucy smiled and grabbed Frankie's arm.

"Okay, okay," he complained. "I don't need the rubbish they're auctioning anyway. Let's go and see Billy. We might even get a cup of tea."

On the way to her car, Lucy wondered if she should call Nick. Would he help her? No, he would simply point out that when things go wrong, people like Frankie will leave you high and dry.

*

In sunny Leygate, Lucy was wondering about a couple of things. Initially, why Frankie had insisted they park the car a fair way from Billy's home. And then, approaching Billy's house, why they made for the little gate at the side and not the front door.

Her phoned pinged.

"You can silence that," Frankie instructed, donning a pair of lightweight gloves.

It was a text from Nick asking if everything was alright. She didn't answer it.

"I scoped it out last night," Frankie said, handing her the small bag he was carrying. "The gate's padlock is twenty seconds."

Lucy didn't get it, but Frankie – amazingly for man of his years – climbed over.

Twenty seconds later, he opened the gate holding the padlock.

"Come on," he advised taking the bag from her.

This was a dark turn. Lucy had never illegally entered

anyone's premises before. Pushing her forward though was the idea that they might discover evidence of Billy's insurance fraud – even though it seemed completely unlikely.

There was another power at work, of course. The need to return home to Barnet with a feeling that absolutely no stone had been left unturned and that the whole thing could be considered concluded for the rest of time.

At the back door, Frankie started on the lock.

"What about the security cameras?" Lucy asked.

"Not working," said Frankie.

"How do you know?"

"I sprayed them with black paint last night."

"Last night?"

"Yeah, I had to wait ages for him to pop to the loo. Then I was in. So, it's a wireless system. That's blocked now though. The interference kit's in the bag."

Frankie opened the door.

"Hang on," said Lucy. "What about Billy?"

"He's meeting someone in Arundel on urgent business. A face from his past tempted him there with the prospect of learning some very important information. He should be meeting him about now."

"This man he's meeting. Do I know him?"

"Yes, it's me."

"You?"

"Obviously, I'm not actually there. But he is."

"You planned this all along. You're only here to steal his stuff."

"I told you we'd get justice by the back door, didn't I? This is the back door."

"*This*... feels wrong."

"Will you step inside before someone sees us?"

Despite the doubts, she followed him into the dining

room.

"If you're here to steal his silver, why are you involving me?"

"I need a second pair of eyes and hands... and an alibi. According to Terry, you work at a theological college. You'll be able to vouch for me if the police poke their noses in. I'll be able to say I was making love with you at your hotel."

"You bloody well will not!"

"We'll say we had a picnic on the Downs then. The main thing is they won't suspect you, so I'll be in the clear."

"I won't allow it. I'm only interested in finding a way to prove Billy Brown committed fraud. Then I'll hand it over to the police."

"No, you won't. They'll target Eddie and the chalice. Your Aunt Libby will have police boots marching through her house before you can say Hawaii Five-O."

Lucy felt trapped. Logic and criminality were ganging up on her.

"Now listen," said Frankie. "Billy Brown has a hoard of genuine silver antiques and we're going to take the lot."

She followed him into the lounge.

"I can't believe it. Why didn't you break in years ago? It would have saved you from a parasitic lifestyle."

"I only recently found out the collection was genuine," said Frankie, admiring the cabinet full of old silver.

Lucy swallowed. "How recently?"

"Yesterday, when you told Terry. I was there with him. Thank you for being on my side, Lucy."

"Yuck. For the record, Billy said he created the fake collection to use as collateral to raise a loan from a loan shark."

"You don't believe that, do you?"

"I'm seriously tempted to call the police. Libby would understand."

"Oh yeah? You like prison food? You're an accessory. You told me the silver was genuine and you told me you wanted to settle a score for your aunt. You even drove me here."

Lucy was beginning to feel ill.

"This is all wrong."

"You really are gullible. You know what he did with the insurance money? He bought real versions of the fakes. Clever man."

He opened the cabinet and picked up the jug.

"I thought you said he started a crime wave with Pleasant Peter?"

"That too."

"Next you'll say he's Jack the Ripper. Why do you hate him?"

Frankie turned to face her.

"He gave my name to the police. I did three years for handling stolen antiques. I tried to get back at him, but he found out and threatened me. It was you who gave me the idea of trying again. He won't be expecting it after all this time."

"But he's expecting to meet you in Arundel."

"Yes, but I'm impersonating Ernie Bright."

"Who's Ernie Bright?"

"A face from the past."

"But Ernie's not there."

"No, of course he's not."

"Does Ernie know he's not there?"

"How could he? I never told him."

She checked her phone again. The text from Nick. What would he think of her now? He wouldn't be too impressed. Even so, she felt like calling him.

"Okay, so it's a two-way split," said Frankie, eyeing up the cabinet. "You can give Libby twenty grand out of your half."

"No, put that jug back and let's go."

"Billy owes her. Eddie wasn't a crook. He got paid for his work with an antique, except it was a fake. Billy stitched both Eddie and me up. He owes us."

"No."

"Come on – we'll celebrate together. I'll show you a good time."

"How dare you. You don't know me at all."

"Yes, I do. You're a pushover. Don't deny it."

"You're an ageing lawbreaker with no morals!"

"True… maybe I'm getting a little old for this kind of thing. Admit it, though – you're tempted."

"You must be deranged. I'd rather tear my right arm off and beat myself senseless with it."

"I'll take that as a possible."

Lucy looked around. What had she got herself into?

He smiled at her.

"You never know when another opportunity might arise," he said. "Your whole life could change right now by not acting like a numpty."

"No, there has to be a better way. What if we take photos of all the silver and then try to match it to… to…?"

"Try to match it to a collection of fakes? …Last seen a million years ago by a bent valuer who's dead, Eddie, who's dead, and Pleasant Peter, who's ninety but definitely worth avoiding?"

"Maybe there are papers…"

"Yeah, maybe he's left a signed letter in a drawer. Whoever so finds this letter, I hereby declare my total guilt as a master criminal. Yours truly, Billy."

"Well, what do you suggest then?"

"I suggest we get even."

"No."

"I'll just take my share then."

"You do and I'll…"

"What? Tell the police?"

"No, I'll tell Billy."

Frankie took a moment then put the jug back.

29

And What Do You Believe?

That afternoon, Lucy went to see Nick. She needed help.

On arrival, she found him busy with a middle-aged male customer, so she began to while away the time studying an item described by the label as a Victorian walnut Canterbury in excellent condition. Circa 1860. £350.

It looked like a magazine rack, which she supposed it was.

She switched to something smaller. A Victorian mother-of-pearl card case. Circa 1850. £135. Ideal for storing modern business cards.

Hmmm.

Next to it was a pair of Victorian opera glasses made by J. H. Steward of Cornhill, London. Nick had them on sale for a hundred. They were lovely, even though the original black leather and scarlet silk-lined case was a little worn. Intriguingly, the initials of the original owner could be seen etched into the metal between the eyepieces.

R. R.

Who was R. R. and did a mystery lie behind the

glasses?

Probably not.

She peered through them to the pharmacy across the street. Not bad. She felt she needed opera glasses. That way she might be able to see what was going on more clearly. She turned around still holding them up. A blurry man was coming toward her.

She lowered the glasses as Nick's customer left with something in a small paper bag.

Nick came over.

"I could do with some advice," she said.

"What kind of advice?"

"According to Frankie, Billy spent years putting together a collection of fake silver antiques. He got a dishonest valuer involved, had everything insured, and then had them stolen. He used the insurance money to fund bigger crime."

"If nothing else, Billy's thorough."

"The thing is – he cheated Uncle Eddie."

"Paying him for services with a fake antique?"

"Yes."

"So, Eddie assumed the cup was genuine?"

"Yes."

"And that's the whole story?"

"No, that's Fast Frankie's story."

"Right."

"Billy's story is that Eddie stole the cup thinking it was genuine. He thinks Eddie was waiting for him to die before selling it. Billy says he never knew it was Eddie who stole it until I told him Libby had a fake silver cup."

"Right, so… is Billy a crook or not?"

"He says he created a collection of fakes to use as collateral to raise a loan from a loan shark. Billy was a convicted crook. He couldn't go to the bank. He paid a shady valuer at a good auction house to value the collection and hold it in storage."

"So, the loan shark was satisfied the collection was real?"

"Yes. Billy says he used the loan to get himself into a legit business. Once he had that, he worked hard to repay the loan. Except Billy couldn't let it be known the collection was fake, as the loan guy would have been annoyed. I'm thinking shoot-your-kneecaps-off annoyed."

"And that's it?"

"Yes."

"Two versions, two possibilities…"

"Yes."

"And what do you believe?"

"My gut instinct is Billy committed an insurance fraud and got involved in bigger crime. I think Eddie was an idiot, but he knew the cup was a fake when he accepted it as payment for whatever services he provided."

"Why hide it in the loft?"

"So that Libby would think it was real and that Eddie was successful."

"So, it all comes back to Billy. He's a long-time villain."

"Yes."

"But he doesn't owe Libby twenty thousand."

"No – but this isn't about money. It's about doing the right thing. Billy's had a good life and I want to bring him down."

"Are you sure? You're a reception manager at a theological college. Your strong point is providing refreshment packages for tired vicars."

"I know. I'm not really sure how to go about it."

"I could ask a friend – Detective Inspector Ian

Crawford. He's the guy whose wife paid two thousand for a fake painting. I now advise her on antiques. He'll be interested in fraud. He'll sniff it out if it's there."

"What if I'm wrong?"

"Sometimes we have to back our judgement."

"Yes… we do."

Two elderly women came in.

"Vases?" one of them asked.

"Certainly, madam," said Nick.

*

That evening, in her hotel room, sitting on the edge of the bed, staring out at the night sky, each minute seeming like ten…

Lucy had already called Jane, who was relieved to hear from her. Jane had tried to get through a couple of times, but, of course, Lucy had rejected her calls. They made a promise to see each other again, and soon. According to Jane, nothing would get in the way of their friendship – and Lucy wanted to believe that.

She also called Victoria, but on hearing her voice, decided that her daughter's sharing of the Leo business didn't need to be mentioned – ever. From what she could piece together, Victoria had told Ellie in the spirit of making her mum, Jane, aware that middle-aged divorcees were a target demographic for romance scam artists.

The call had instead focused on happier things and ended with Lucy reassuring Victoria that she was tying up a few loose ends and would be back home on Sunday afternoon, and back at work on Monday morning.

Long after the call, she pondered the question.

What next?

Lucy wasn't sure what she was doing, but she was

doing it anyway. Nick's friendly detective inspector was okay for a call on Billy in the morning.

So, in her hotel room, sitting on the edge of the bed, staring out at the night sky, it appeared that everything was set.

She glanced at her watch.

10:05 p.m.

Nick would be with Jane.

30

Surprises

Sunday morning. A time for staying in bed. Or strolling with a pet dog.

Lucy was outside Billy Brown's house with Nick and an unconvinced Detective Inspector Ian Crawford. She almost laughed. She had come to Sussex armed with the surefire knowledge that getting sucked into other people's problems only ever ended badly.

And now...?

"I can't say I'm happy about this," said Crawford, ringing the doorbell. "I'm not a big fan of dusty old cases."

"Hopefully, he'll confess," said Nick. "Or at least give you enough signs that he's guilty."

"I'm sure it'll be straightforward," said Lucy.

"Nothing's straightforward," said Crawford. "Otherwise decent people would be able to buy antiques without getting stitched up."

A moment later, a puzzled-looking Billy Brown opened the door.

"My birthday's not till next month."

"Don't give me any of that," said Crawford. "I'm assuming you're Billy Brown?"

"And I'm assuming you're a cop. What's this about?"

"I'm Detective Inspector Crawford and I'm making some preliminary enquiries into a suspected fraud case. Would you be so kind as to put the kettle on and provide some answers?"

"Do you have a warrant?"

"I have no intention of searching you or your home, I simply have a slight headache from a late night and would appreciate some public-spirited coffee."

Billy glanced at Lucy.

"I knew you'd be trouble."

He turned inside and disappeared into the hall, leaving the door open.

A few minutes later, they were all seated in the lounge with instant coffee in cheap mugs.

"You look pleased," Billy said to Lucy.

But she wasn't pleased. The look on her face was more likely anxiety. But she would push through it and get to the truth. That wasn't in question. Libby wouldn't be getting any money, but at least Billy Brown would be held to account.

"Let's cut through all the niceties," said Crawford. "Lucy, you dragged me here – why don't you remind us what's what."

Lucy stood up and paced to the window before turning. She wasn't sure why, although it did seem an approach that was popular with TV detectives bringing their cases to a conclusion. Certainly, Poirot seemed to enjoy it.

"I think I know everything," she said. "Billy, you spent years putting together a collection of fake silver antiques. You got a dishonest valuer involved, you had everything insured, and then you arranged to have the collection stolen. We can come to what you did with the insurance money later."

Billy nodded. "And you got this information from Fast Frankie?"

"Yes, but I believe it's true."

"And did Frankie mention which insurance company I defrauded?"

Lucy was ready for that one. "This would have been decades ago, long before things went online. It would take a long time to track it down, but the police will if you won't tell us."

Crawford sighed. "Billy, the idea is that you confess and save me a lot of paperwork. Can you recall the name of the insurance provider you defrauded?"

Billy eyed Lucy. "Is this really down to your aunt finding her cup wasn't a genuine antique?"

"Yes, first there was the cup, and then Eddie's connection to you…"

Lucy was searching for a way to frame her conclusion, because at that moment she knew she was on the right track. As she considered her approach, her gaze alighted on a photo on the wall beside the fireplace. It was young Billy with the racing car called Rocket.

Except…

Billy knew all about the Howards…

He knew because…

She studied the photo more closely.

"Everything okay?" Nick asked.

"Yes, it's…"

But something, somewhere in Lucy's brain had clicked. That first time she came into this room, he didn't call the car 'rocket', he said it 'went like a rocket'.

She had a bad feeling.

The photo. The car. Its name painted on the side. Roc... with the rest of the word hidden behind the handsome young man...

"This car..." She turned to Billy. "Is it called Rocinante?"

"Yes, it is," said Billy.

"Do what?" said Crawford.

"Yes, so," Lucy continued, "is that a young you?"

"No, it's not."

"Then is it a cousin of a woman called Virginia Kirby."

"Yes, it's Ray Flynn. He's my cousin too."

Lucy felt her grip on reality beginning to slip. What did it mean?

Inspector Crawford huffed.

"Can I ask where this is getting us? From where I'm sitting, I'd say we're hurtling at top speed to nowhere."

But Lucy's focus was on Billy.

"So... you're related to Virginia?"

"She's my sister."

Lucy gulped. "Oh my..."

"How else did you think she got in touch with you? I told her you'd paid me a visit. It took her bloody ages to find one of your posters. I wish I hadn't bothered now."

Lucy's brain was rapidly trying to rearrange everything. She felt like a victim of a TV prank show.

"Okay, okay... give me a second... so Ray Flynn knew Ned-Rocinante long before Libby did."

Crawford growled. "Unless Ned Rocinante is a mafia hitman, I'm off. There's a bacon roll at home with my name on it."

"We were all close family," said Billy. "Ray lost his mum in an air raid when he was a baby. She'd gone to the cinema with my grandad's sister for a few hours of respite... After the War, Ray lived with his dad, but we grew up like brothers. Did you know your Aunt Libby nearly married him?"

Lucy took a breath. "Ray and Libby?"

Inspector Crawford cracked. "Okay, what the effin' 'eck is going on?"

"It's my fault," said Lucy. "When I said I knew everything, I was actually completely wrong. Don't worry, it's all rushing into my head now."

"What are you on? Crack cocaine?"

Lucy stared out of the rear window to the garden.

"We have to call this off."

"Call it off?"

"Yes, I'm sure Billy's innocent."

"What? You are seriously close to big trouble."

"Hang on, Ian," said Nick, "she can explain. You can explain, can't you?"

"If you don't explain," Crawford gasped, "I'll have you down the station for wasting my Sunday morning. And believe me, that's a very serious charge."

Despite feeling light-headed, Lucy faced him down.

"Billy and Virginia are brother and sister. Ray the racing driver was their cousin. They all had a rocking horse called Rocinante. The horse became Ned, owned by Sylvia, Eleanor and then Libby. Ray later drove a racing car called Rocinante. Libby fell in love with him. I'm assuming there was an age difference?"

"Seven years," said Billy.

Crawford looked set to explode.

"So bloody what?"

Tears filled Billy's eyes.

"My cousin and best friend. He was going to marry your aunt Libby. She was only eighteen…"

"What happened?" asked Crawford. "Did he die in a crash?"

"Ray's not dead," fumed Billy. "He lives in Bognor."

"Same thing," Crawford huffed.

Lucy considered it. "I'm guessing the Howard family put a stop to it because they held Ray in low regard. His cousins were servants to the Howards."

Billy nodded. "Ray ended up running a boat hire business, but he retired when his wife died. It's just him and his dog now."

"I'm not interested in this twaddle," said Crawford. He eyeballed Lucy. "How does any of this prove this man is innocent of defrauding an insurance company?"

But Lucy was certain.

"My instincts are now that Billy is honest. An awkward man, but a good one."

"Because he had a horse and a racing driver cousin?" Crawford turned to Nick. "She is half an inch from being arrested for wasting police time."

"I believe Billy's version," Lucy insisted. "He created a fake collection and had a dishonest valuer value them. They were good quality fakes. There were a lot of them about in those days. All made for the Edwardian years when there was plenty of money."

"Spare me the history lesson," said Crawford.

"Billy used the collection as collateral for a loan... and used the loan to create a legitimate business."

"At last, someone's talking sense," said Billy.

"It sounds completely implausible," said Crawford.

"It's not," said Lucy. "He did so because he had a criminal record. He had no choice. It was either bend the rules or spend his life bemoaning his lot."

She felt a little awkward about that last point.

"Perhaps Billy should start at the beginning," said Nick.

"Yes, well, keep it short," huffed Crawford.

"It's my turn to speak, is it?" said Billy. "Okay, once upon a time I lived in a lovely cottage."

"Don't take the piss," Crawford insisted.

"Okay, but it *was* a lovely cottage…"

31

More Surprises

"My earliest memory is when I was five years old," said Billy. "I was planting things in the little front garden of our place in Camley, and there was my grandad coming along the street with a creaky old handcart. And on it, our rocking horse. It had gone from my sister to my cousin, and now it was coming back home to me. In all my years, I've never been happier than at that moment."

Crawford groaned.

"Give him a chance," said Nick.

"A couple of years later, we lost everything. We had to leave our cottage because Mum owed so much in rent to Sir George. He even took the horse and gave it to his granddaughter. He told her it was a top-class antique specimen."

"Nice man," said Nick.

"Until Lucy turned up, me and my sister had no idea where the horse was. We didn't want to ask any of the Howards. We promised ourselves a long time ago we wouldn't rely on them for anything."

"I don't blame you," said Lucy.

"In fact, the last time I relied on them was in the early sixties when I left the army after National Service. My sister was working for Sir George as a servant and got me a job there as a gardener. It came to quite an abrupt end though."

"What happened?" asked Crawford.

"He died."

"Did you murder him?"

"No."

"There's less and less for me to do here, isn't there."

"The Howards were always being charitable," said Billy, "or so they thought. They had the best of us and they even took my horse. We had to work hard for little in return and were never left in any doubt of the Howards' superiority. I remember one day, I must have been nine… Sir George was reminding my mum that his family were helping my family with a roof over our heads. By that he meant a single room in a grotty house. Being a fair-minded boy, I stepped forward and promised him that if his family ever fell on hard times, I'd help them with a roof over *their* heads. He laughed and told me not to be so silly. But that only made me more determined to keep to my word."

"So, the legit business?" said Lucy.

"Property," said Billy. "A respected company called Charterhouse."

"Wow," said Lucy.

"The first property I bought was our old cottage with the yellow clematis I planted as a boy. I still pay someone to tend the front and back gardens today, even though it's rented to a lovely senior citizen."

"Oh my," gasped Lucy. "Libby lives in your old home."

"Yes, fully renovated and restored with an added

garage and a new clematis. Moving Libby and Eddie there in the nineties without them knowing I owned it was a satisfying day for me. It took some leg work and the lowest rent on the market, but they were desperate."

Lucy let it seep in. "Did you help Sylvia and Eleanor, too… without letting them know?"

"Yes, I did, after Eddie lost all their money. A promise is a promise."

"It's extraordinary," said Lucy.

"You make it sound grand, but it started with a need to be in a position where no one would ever take my home away from me again. Of course, the business did grow over time – to thirty-five properties."

"That's amazing," said Lucy. "Truly amazing."

"Yes, yippee and hoorah," said Crawford. "So that's everything."

"Not everything," said Lucy. "Someone stole a silver cup."

"At last, a crime. Who stole it?"

"No one," said Billy. "It was all a misunderstanding. There was no theft and no crime."

He winked at Lucy.

Crawford got to his feet.

"Nick, we're even. In fact, you owe me."

A moment later, they heard the front door close behind him.

Billy stood up.

"Fresh air, anyone?"

Lucy and Nick were soon on the patio with him. There was a plane high overhead. And birdsong.

They each took a seat at the wrought iron outdoor table, with Lucy still concerned about one aspect of the affair.

"Will you go after Frankie?" she asked.

"No," said Billy. "He's a waste of time and effort. He'll disappear back down the sewer."

"Why does he hate you so much?" Nick asked.

"His jail term was for theft of an antique silver dinner plate. I'd stupidly told people I was buying it and left it with a valuer – a proper one. Then it went missing. Frankie thought I'd given his name to the police, but I didn't know he'd stolen it. Of course, I'd already put out the word that I was onto the rat who nicked my chalice, even though I had no idea."

Lucy understood.

"So, Eddie believed – wrongly – that you were closing in on him. To keep you off the scent, he got Frankie arrested for the silver plate to make you think Frankie was also behind the chalice theft."

"Yeah, it did make me think Frankie possibly took the chalice, but I moved on. He came after me a while later, saying I'd given him up to the police and demanding two grand in compensation. I explained that he should depart forthwith and if I even heard his name again, I'd end his days with immediate effect. The little coward ran off and that was that. To be honest, I wasn't interested in getting bogged down in a pool of scum inhabited by the likes of Frankie and, as I now know, Eddie."

Lucy thought of her aunt. "Libby won't want to know any of this."

"She chose the wrong man," said Billy. "Ray was a good 'un, Eddie was a lazy loser."

"Great photo," said Lucy. "With the car."

"He drove for a rich man. It was an expensive sport. Still is, of course."

"He got to name the car though."

"Only for the last race of the season. It was booked in for a respray, so why not. It was around that time I introduced him to Libby. There's a picture of her sitting in the car, but I don't know what became of it."

"That I would *love* to see," said Lucy.

"Well, all's well that ends well," said Nick.

Lucy could only marvel at Billy. "To think the Howards now pay you rent."

"Poetic," said Nick.

"I'm a good landlord," said Billy. "I would never hold someone's family background against them."

Lucy appreciated the irony.

"You're retired now, I expect," said Nick.

"Yeah, kind of. My son-in-law runs it these days. I'm under doctor's orders to put my feet up and avoid stress – so thanks for the home invasion, harassment, and police investigation."

"I'm really sorry," said Lucy. "And that's on behalf of all the Howards."

"It's okay. The Howards' rent pays my retirement income, so in a way the Howards are looking after me. We can't do without each other."

Lucy rose to her feet.

"Keep well," she said. "And I promise to stay out of your life."

"Yeah, well, you can stay in it a bit longer," said Billy. "I need you to get on a ladder and clean the paint off my security cameras."

32

So…

Lucy brought the hire car to a halt outside Libby's house. This would be the first of her little chats with family members. Before heading home, she would see Eleanor and Jane too. The healing needed to begin, and Lucy would be the first to say sorry.

She turned to her passenger.

"Ten days ago, I came back to Sussex for Libby's birthday. She was wondering why her chalice wasn't real."

"And now you have the answer," said Nick.

"My grandad Tommy Holt always said behind every antique, there's a story. He used to say look for it because it makes all the difference. He said it applied to people too."

"Maybe he was hoping one day you'd take a closer look at the Howards."

A few minutes later, they were in the lounge with Libby, sipping tea and munching on chocolate fingers.

Libby had news.

"My landlord's been in touch," she declared.

"On a Sunday?" said Lucy.

"Yes, the man at their office said they were about to buy smaller properties in new areas to expand the business. One of the places they'll be buying a cottage or bungalow is Selsey."

"Isn't that where…?" But Lucy didn't get a chance to finish.

"…My best friend lives? Yes. The landlord was calling me on the off chance I might fancy a change. And, you'll never believe this, but the rent would be specially discounted for my inconvenience!"

Nick laughed. "What a lovely landlord you have."

Lucy was happy for her aunt. Maybe now wasn't the time for truth.

"I'm sorry I didn't find out much about Eddie and the chalice," she said.

"Oh, that's alright," said Libby. "You're a regular Saint Jude – our very own patron saint of lost causes."

"I'm really not a saint."

"You never got to the bottom of who gave Eddie the chalice, but you never stopped trying."

"Yes, well, the most likely explanation is that Eddie simply trusted too many people."

"It's all water under the bridge now, but it's ended well. I couldn't be happier."

"That's the main thing."

"Of course, Eleanor's decided against writing up the family history, but I expect it's for the best."

"Hmm… on other matters, I'd like to sort out Ned's future. Could I buy him from you?"

"I think that's a sensible solution," said Libby. "But what price should we place on a genuine Victorian rocking horse. Didn't you tell me they go for five thousand?"

"Only the very finest," Nick interjected.

"I could go to two thousand," said Lucy, hoping Libby wouldn't ask for more.

"Nonsense," said Libby. "I won't accept a penny."

Lucy was taken aback. "Are you sure?"

"Yes, I'm sure."

"Thank you."

Libby turned to Nick. "But I *would* like to get some money for the chalice... if you're still interested. Six hundred?"

"Oh, er... call it five-fifty?"

Lucy avoided Nick's gaze. She had just cost him fifty pounds.

*

After tea, Lucy left the car at Libby's and headed for the High Street on foot with Nick.

"Will you ever tell Libby the truth?" he asked.

"Probably... possibly... but I want her to move to Selsey first."

"Ah, the Howard pride. She'd no doubt refuse her landlord's help if she knew Billy was behind it."

"Once she's settled there, I'll ask Jane what she thinks. No rush, though. I think we'll put Libby's happiness first and foremost."

Nick's phoned pinged. While he dealt with a text, Lucy looked back on her Sussex adventure. Nick getting involved by saying he knows a man... not on his official list...

Her asking if they could discuss Aunt Libby... Him smiling and saying they had discussed little else.

Him holding an impromptu auction just for her. "What am I bid? A bone china Queen Elizabeth the Second coronation cup and saucer. Do I hear one pound?" And her feeling a fool but wanting to break through her wall of reserve so badly.

Him advising that you never phone if you want information. It's far better to see the whites of their eyes. You'll spot a lie straight away.

Her saying she and Ned went after the bad guys. And him simply saying, "Tell me more."

Him saying to the property guy… "If you could give me the address, my wife and I would like to get on with the rest of our weekend."

Her wondering if he went to bed dressed like Scrooge…

Nick tucked his phone away as they headed into the heart of the town.

"Where will you store the horse?" he asked.

"I'm not keeping him."

"No?"

"I just need to make a quick call."

She called Virginia.

"I've got Rocinante for you. He's all yours, back where he belongs. Shall we arrange a delivery time?"

"Lucy, I'm overwhelmed. My old Rocinante. We must have covered thousands of miles together. I can't take him back though."

"But he's yours. You must."

"No, he's yours now. It doesn't matter if he's called Ned. As long as he's with someone who loves him, that's all that matters."

"He spent thirty years in a garage under a sheet."

"But you're going to change all that."

Lucy thought about that for a moment.

"Yes. If you're sure… then, yes, I am."

She ended the call as they reached the High Street.

"It looks like I'm keeping him."

"That's great. If he needs a temporary home, he's welcome to stay with me. We could hang a 'sold' tag from his ear and you could come and visit."

Lucy didn't answer.

"Um… on other things," said Nick. "I didn't see Jane last night."

Lucy felt a jolt.

"Was she ill?"

"No."

"Were you ill?"

"No."

"Did the restaurant burn down?"

"No."

"I see."

"I'm sorry things got messed up. I wish they hadn't."

"That's life, I suppose."

"I wasn't looking for a relationship. That door was bolted shut. It's just… you kind of opened things up again. I realized I wasn't happy on my own…"

"I left. I wasn't planning to come back."

"But Ned had other ideas?"

"That horse interferes far too often."

"He's got quite a pedigree, hasn't he."

"Yes, built by Henry Stafford in 1943… during the War… what a brilliant grandad he must have been."

They stepped aside to let a family with three children through. The smallest child was riding a bicycle with stabilizers.

"Remind me of Ned's owners again," said Nick.

"It's just a list of children between six and eight years. Except those are such special years when we still believe in magic. The impossible is the everyday. I've got all the dates and all the names. Virginia, Ray, Billy, Sylvia, Eleanor, Libby, Richard, me, Jane, Simon, Keith, Libby's garage, and now me again."

"That's what I call a five-star provenance."

"Well, he's not technically an antique."

"Twenty years from now, he will be. And you'll have the whole story, all the names, and all the dates. It's an antique collector's dream."

"I'll never let him go again. Now I have Virginia's blessing, he's staying with me."

"But you will let him go one day. It's decided by Time. We can't alter that. The only bit we can affect is what comes next. Today. Tomorrow. Next week."

"Yes... I'll write down Ned Rocinante's story. The true version."

"Do you think Ned Rocinante has more adventures lined up?" Nick wondered.

But Lucy had her future mapped out, planned, decided. It was back home, back to work, back to her comfortable existence.

"What about the future," Nick asked, pausing at the door to Taylor's Antiques.

"The scary one or the easy one?"

"The scary one."

"It depends..."

"On what?"

"People."

Something had changed. Not in the world. In her.

They went inside to the tinkle of the bell above the door.

"Hello, you two," said Fay, peering up from a magazine in the absence of customers.

"Almost closing time," said Nick. He reached for the open/close sign and turned it over.

"Coffee?" Fay offered.

"Yes please," Nick and Lucy chimed together.

Fay went out the back, leaving Lucy to wonder what Nick might say. Would she end up being the fool once again?

"How about over there for the horse?" He was pointing to a good spot below a window. "He'll make that section look more interesting."

"Great," said Lucy.

"I'm glad you're keeping him. All those wonderful memories…"

"We used to go after the bad guys," she reminded him.

"Every day a great adventure?"

"Yes, like Don Quixote riding Rocinante. Those two have reminded me that adventure is the spice of life. I'm not very good at it, but…"

"…but Don Quixote teaches us that there is worth in all of us, regardless of who we are or where we come from."

"Yes."

"…and that if we follow antiquated beliefs, we might not find the best way for ourselves."

"You've read it."

"I have a first edition upstairs."

"Hey, if you had a first edition of the world's first ever modern novel, you would be the richest man in England."

"True – maybe it's a copy. I wondered why there was a Penguin on the spine."

She wanted to be with him.

"Are you really interested in adventure?" he asked.

"I told you, I'm not very good at it."

"I've seen the photo of you and Ned. You looked pretty good at it back then. In my opinion, you never really lose it. It's just a question of practice."

"Do you think so?"

"A client of mine has acquired a painting – an 1899 Ferdinand Roybet called 'The Drunken Cavalier with Two Maids'. It's not one that's come to light before and I think it might have been stolen from an estate near Chichester thirty years ago. I said I'd try to find out a bit more before we talk to the police. Would you be interested in helping me?"

"Me?"

"Yes… intrepid, inspiring you."

"Well… they say behind every antique, there's a story."

"Yes, they do."

"So…" she uttered.

"So?"

"I suppose I could take some more time off work. A week or two." Her heart pounded. This was the moment. "Should I get a room in Camley so that I'm nearer?"

He smiled with such warmth as he held his arms open.

And despite all the fears and doubts, all the likely upheaval, Lucy placed her trust in him. And stepped into his embrace. Into a different future.

The End

Thank you for reading Lucy Holt Gets Involved.

I have a small request. I'm not a big-name author, so it's hard work getting people to take a chance on my books. I don't have a multi-national publishing corporation spreading the word for me, so I'm reliant on good people like yourself to help me. If you enjoyed this book, I would be forever grateful if you could leave a review on Amazon. I know it's a pesky nuisance, but it's how lesser-known authors like me can gain traction for our books (which means we can write more books). It would make me incredibly happy if you were able to say something nice in the review.

For more info about me and my books, and to sign up for my newsletter, pop across to my website:

www.markdaydy.co.uk

Thanks,
Mark

Printed in Great Britain
by Amazon